The Summer of Tsunami, Lega

Copyright © 2012 by S. Cam̃pbell Wĩ̃lĩ̃ams, ̃ ̃ ̃ ̃roup

ISBN-13:
978-1506005492

ISBN-10:
1506005497

Cover photo courtesy of S. Campbell Williams
Copyright © 2014 by S. Campbell Williams, Dionne Media Group

Dedication

This novel is dedicated to my Grandmother, Eva May. Thank you for all the love and support you gave me in my youth, for never turning family away and letting me be myself, without question. Your stability gave me strength.

Foreword

I consider myself to be a storyteller, and the *Legacy* series is the first of my stories to be told. Coming from a family with many generations of interracial coupling; the initial story came to me when I thought about the issues my predecessors might've encountered in their relationships. Towards the completion of the first book, I found myself drawn to the lives of other characters, and the turmoil of their stories began unraveling. Resulting, is this unique series that ties the reader to individual characters, as well as the entire story as a whole. *The Summer of Tsunami* is the first installment of this tale.

The Summer of Tsunami

Prologue

Lily watched as Elizabeth traced her fingers across Lily's awards and plaques. The bright-eyed girl was fascinated by her older cousin's accomplishments. Elizabeth hoped that one day she'd also become an award winning journalist like Lily. Lily smiled as she recalled idolizing someone like that once. She appreciated Elizabeth's candor, and even though they were cousins, Lily was respected as her Great Aunt.

"Have I given you everything you need to complete your report, Elizabeth?" Lily asked.

"I think so. You've led such an amazing life, Auntie Lily. I sure hope I get to see the world as you have."

"I'm sure you will do whatever and go wherever your heart leads you," Lily suggested. "You've got lots of time still. Fifteen's nowhere near the end of your days. Just stay focus on what you want, dear."

"Auntie Lily, out of all the stories you reported, which is the one you remember most? Your favorite?" Elizabeth inquired. Lily paused and silently contemplated the answer for a moment.

"My favorite story is one that I never reported."

"Why not?" Elizabeth inquired.

"Because it would've hurt people that I love and hold dear to my heart, to publish the beautiful and ugly truths of their lives." Lily paused, looking into Elizabeth's confused face. "It is your story. The story of you, child."

"I don't understand, Auntie Lily."

"I'm talking bout how you came to be. The very reason you exist. Your story rooted something over seventy, eighty years ago. But I will only tell it to you in the order I uncovered it," Lily stated. "Would you like to know your story?" Elizabeth was intrigued. She possessed the same curiosity and hunger for information that Lily did.

"I would," she replied.

"I'm glad to hear you say that. See that frame on the wall?" Lily pointed to her wall covered with plaques. "The one with the worn out letter in it. Bring it to me." Elizabeth scanned the frames until she found the right one. She handed it over to Lily.

"This is what started your story for me. It's been fifty plus years since I first saw this letter, but I remember it all like it was yesterday." Lily took the wrinkled letter out of the frame and began to flashback, as she read it aloud to Elizabeth.

June 1, 1961

Dearest Sister,

Thank you so much for agreeing to have Tsu stay with you and your family for the summer, while the CT house is being renovated. I will be departing with my employer and most treasured friend, Mrs. Ellington on June 15th for our European vacation. We will be returning before Labor Day and will meet Tsu at the bus station in New York before returning to Connecticut. I pray that this time with your family in Virginia will be good for Tsu. As you know that incident that occurred some years back now, just about broke my baby girl. Although she has accomplished much, she is but a spark

6

of the girl I remember. And in more recent events, since that scoundrel of an ex-fiancé of hers left her for another woman last year, she has been more reserved than usual. Most of her time is spent with her nose deep in a book or writing stories she doesn't have the courage to pursue publishing.

I am thankful that Mrs. Ellington showed her how to make soap. At least it gives the poor girl something else to do and to interact some with the real world. Also give my thanks to James for arranging for Tsu's soaps to be sold while she is there for the summer. And for volunteering your daughter to be Tsu's assistant. Being around people will be good for her. She gets overwhelmed easily, especially around men so have James keep an eye on her. I know you think I fuss too much over my grown daughter, but I worry that she isn't anywhere close to being her true self. Remember what Daddy use to say? Living a half-life or a life without finding your purpose is almost like being dead. My girl's got more spirit than that. I just don't know what else to do to get her going.

Anyways, she should be arriving in Lexington on Friday at 4:45 p.m. I threw away all of her old maid clothes, gave her some of my old ones and made some new ones as well. Don't you go bout getting any ideas bout fitting into any of my old dresses either! They are for Tsu and Tsu only. Besides I don't believe your hips will be able to fit in anything of mine anymore.

Take good care of my baby. She is a good girl and will help you in any way you need. See that she gets out once and a while. I hope that those books aren't the only adventure she has this summer.

Love you Swirly and thanks again.

Anne Monroe

Lily watched her mother fold the letter from her Auntie Anne back into thirds and tuck it into its envelope. Tomorrow her cousin would be arriving from Connecticut to stay with her family for the summer. Surely Auntie Anne didn't expect Lily's mother to babysit a grown woman, insecure or not. Shirley and Jimmy had decided that they wouldn't fuss over the girl at all. They would leave it to their younger daughter Lily to show Tsu around the town. The family thought that the best thing for the girl would be for her to find her own adventures, instead of having one put in place for her. However, they would indeed make sure that Tsu got out to a few of the social functions, as requested by her mother.

Lily kissed her mother and father good night before, Shirley turned out the light next to her bed. Tomorrow would be a big day for the Gaines Family. They hadn't seen Tsu, since she was a thirteen years old girl, but she was family. Lily knew that her parents were never ones to turn away family when or if anyone needed it. As soon as she hit her bed, Lily drifted off to sleep, thinking about the meal she would help her mother prepare for tomorrow's dinner.

Chapter One

It was just before the summer of 1961 in Lexington, Virginia. Main Street had a mild amount of activity for an early spring evening. It was Friday, and the weekends always brought about the town's weekly baseball games. At precisely five o'clock the store owners would hustle to close down their shops. Lexington would practically become a ghost town for the weekend games out at the old baseball fields.

Inside of Baker's General Store, Lily spied tall, slender, graying Mr. Baker through the screen door. He was overseeing an employee sweeping out the store for the evening. Out of the corner of his eye, Mr. Baker caught hold of the little brown skinned, brown eyed girl as well sitting outside his store. Not paying much mind to the skinny child, he simply nodded at her and continued on with his supervising. The both of them were waiting for the last bus of the day to arrive from Richmond. Lily was excited to meet her cousin and Mr. Baker was waiting to close down his store for the night.

It was early in the month of June, so the heat of the upcoming summer was still building. Lily sat impatiently in her denim shorts and yellow t-shirt on the steps, kicking her lanky legs back and forth. She was beyond anxious while she waited for the 4:45 P.M. bus to pull in. Her parents had charged her with retrieving her older cousin Tsu, off of the bus and to the butcher shop where Lily's father was working. Tsu would be staying with them for the next two and a half months, while her mother was out of the country. Lily could not

9

contain her excitement at the thought of having her cousin around, even though she was almost twice her age. Lily imagined that they'd be the best of friends. Mid-thought, Lily was abruptly interrupted.

"Hey Lil' Bits!" a tall, golden haired, blue-eyed man called out, interrupting Lily's thoughts. "Whatcha doing here outside my daddy's store?" he asked approaching. She jumped up, ready to brawl at the sight of William J. Baker. He was with a couple of his buddies, who were half-dressed in their gray and red baseball gear. She assumed William was looking to pester her as usual.

"I's already toldja Willy J. Baker," Lily hollered. "My name's Lily!" she scowled, placing her boney hands on her fourteen year old hips. She moved closer, down and off of a step at Baker's General Store, until she stood right in front of his lean chest. William placed one of his long legs on the step, leaning into Lily, so that they were eye to eye. "And what I'm doin' here ain't nunna yur bizness." William laughed. He got an immense amount of pleasure out of riling Lily up every chance he got. But it also annoyed him that she would sass him as much as she did. Especially since she was a colored girl. He thought that a colored girl at her age should've known better by now.

"Well, Lil' Bits...," he made certain to emphasize each word. "If ya didn't have such lil' parts, I wouldn't call ya that," he chuckled. A few of his friends, who were standing close by, laughed along with him. "And you are technically on my property. So, I expect for you to show me some respect. Or I reckon I can take you over my knee 'til you can learn to mind your manners, gal." He fully expected the flimsy brown girl to cower before him and to succumb to his intimidating will. Lily's face scrunched up real tight, her dark brown eyes becoming small and sharp. In a low tempting voice she whispered;

"Like ta see ya try." She rolled her eyes hard at him.

"Why you little..."

A fire rose in William's body from Lily's disobedience. William raised his broad hand to strike Lily's relentless face. In an instant, Paul Morrison jumped in the way. He caught hold of William's wrist, before it was about to descend.

"WHOA NOW!" Paul exclaimed, while holding his friend back. "Lily, you starting trouble again?" he asked her while looking into William's agitated blue eyes. Paul's efforts were not to embarrass his friend, but to make it seem like Lily had goaded him. All the while, he was actually saving her from a whooping.

William regained his composure and laughed the incident between her and him off. Still, he didn't appreciate that she had almost made him lose control.

Paul handed her some loose change he pulled from his left pocket. "Here is..." Paul counted the coins in his left hand in a hurry. "Thirteen cents, Lily. Why don't you go get yourself some candy or something, before I knock some sense into you." Paul nodded towards the general store and Lily grabbed the money from Paul's callused hand. Turning a foot, she rolled her brazen eyes at William in the process. Her sass, however intriguing to him, left a bitter taste in William's mouth. Lily was downright rude and disrespectful and William couldn't tolerate anyone besting him.

Paul on the other hand, liked Lily's spunk and he knew her family well. He had done an inordinate amount of carpentry work in the colored neighborhoods in Lexington. It was there that he learned a great deal of his woodworking skill and had gained many colored friends over the years. He didn't want to see any harm come to Lily, especially not at the hand of his good friend Willy J., who was driven to aggravate the poor girl every chance he got. The four men turned from the store, waiting for traffic to clear before crossing. Paul noticed the irritation still residing in William's face, so he threw a friendly arm around his friend's neck and pulled him close.

"Easy buddy. Were you really bout to strike an 80 lb. girl?" Paul joked, playing the incident down, trying to distract William from his anger.

"Nah. I just like to scare some sense in her now and again," William lied. His palm was burning, still itching to redden her small dark face. "Woo-wee though, she's got some balls on her that's for sure. Too much spirit I'd say for a girl, especially a colored gal." His pensive eyes continued to glance in the direction of the general store in which Lily had gone into. He was waiting for her to reappear, as he continued to change into his baseball gear. "Someone needs to whip that gal into her place and soon." William brought his hands to his chest. "And I think I should make it my personal mission to rid her of her current defiant disposition," he explained to his friends in jest.

They all laughed, feeling that William had fallen back into his more charming self.

The initial smirk from William's comment began to fade from Paul's face. For a moment, he found himself bothered by what William's actual intentions might be towards little Lily Gaines.

"You should be less concerned with little girls and more concerned with beating the *Alabaster All-stars* in tonight's game, Willy J.", Paul reminded his friend. He hoped to distract William's thoughts. The four men stood beside Randy Mucker's powder blue car, loading in their baseball gear and buttoning up their uniforms.

William, Paul, Randy and Greg grew up with each other, and had been close friends since they were little boys. William was the alpha male of the group. At the very least, he liked thinking he was. He wouldn't have it any other way. Paul didn't care much about being the leader. He had his hands full most of the time, trying to keep the rest of them out of trouble. They all considered Paul to be the *'Goody Two Shoes'* out of the four of them. But they appreciated it when his good sense saved their hides, as it had done so many times before. Randy and Greg, since childhood, were just tagging along for the William Baker ride.

~   ~   ~   ~   ~

Lily quickly picked out several pieces of red licorice, her favorite, in order to get right back out in front to greet Tsu off of the bus. Lily thought about how she was rather fond of Paul and how handsome she thought he was. He'd always been nice to her, but she couldn't quite understand why he was friends with a jerk like William Baker. With everything that she had heard about Willy J. Baker, Lily couldn't understand why anyone liked him at all.

After paying for her sweet candy, Lily walked through the rickety screen door of the general store. She spied the boys across the steamy concrete road, casually laughing and talking. William's eyes were fixed on Lily as soon as she exited the store. Lily stepped slowly off of the steps of Baker's General Store. She eyed William the entire time, making sure to clear his property.

"I see you, Lil' Bits!" William called out with a half-smile on his face from across the road. He leaned back against Randy's blue car. "And I don't mind waitin' to see what you're up to either," he chuckled with his friends, and he shot her a mischievous wink. Lily rolled her eyes hard at him once again, and continued to chew the sweet sticky red licorice.

~   ~   ~   ~   ~

The Richmond bus began pulling in, momentarily blocking William's relentless gaze. A whirlwind of rust colored dirt swirled about before the bus came to a stop outside of Baker's General Store.

"Lexington, Virginia!" the bus driver called out. "If anyone needs anythang to drink or eat before we depart at 5 o'clock, the general store is still open for the next 10 minutes or so." The driver

14

began to unload the baggage for the Lexington bound passengers. One by one passengers began stepping off the warm bus into the red clouded haze, in search of some refreshment from the general store. Lily sat wide eyed with her mouth slightly parted. She gazed at all the passengers as they climbed off the bus, trying to locate her cousin whom she had never met before. All that Lily knew about Tsu was that she was more than a decade older than herself. She was from Hartford, Connecticut and that Lily would have company for the next two and a half months.

The dust began to clear. Fancy white and black high-heeled shoes stepped out and down onto the rust coated pavement at the bus stop. Legs wrapped in nude stockings led up to a calf-length navy flared skirt, with a white striped blouse perfectly tucked into place. Brown pin up curls cascaded down from under her brimmed white hat. Lily's lips parted a bit further and she took a swallow of air. She hadn't quite gotten a good look at the face of the woman in stripes standing before her.

"Are you Tsu? Cousin Tsu?" she asked the pretty, fancy lady that floated off the bus.

"I am," Tsu answered, as she lifted and set her golden brown eyes on her younger cousin's face. "And you must be Lily. My very own personal assistant for the summer." Lily nodded, mesmerized by Tsu's appearance. Lily was not accustomed to seeing coloreds dressed so business professional. Tsu bent over slightly to get a better look into Lily's bright youthful face. "I must admit, you look absolutely perfect for the job," she admonished. "It's going to be a lot of hard work. Are you sure you're up for it?"

"I is, Tsu. Wait and see. I's good at lotso thangs."

"Hmmmm." Tsu's face tensed. "Your grammar could use some work though. We'll have to include some lessons into *our* work, I'd say," Tsu added. The two continued on with some small talk. Unbeknownst to the young ladies, William, Paul, Randy and Greg caught a glimpse of Tsu's frame. They were awestricken by the woman in navy and stripes that had just stepped into town.

"Holy shit, Randy!" Greg said, tapping Randy on his shoulder. "What in the hell is that?"

"I'm not rightly sure, but it's certainly built for drivin'." Randy answered back taking a thorough scan of the woman's figure beside the bus. William and Paul had noticed her as well, but they momentarily speechless. Never one to miss an opportunity, William quickly regained his wit, and broke his silence.

"Gentlemen, why don't we go over and introduce ourselves to Lil' Bits' friend?" he stammered out. William calmly strode across the road, leading the pack. His eyes were set firmly on the lightly colored, colored girl, conversing with scrawny Lily Gaines. Lily was in the middle of a giggle when William presented himself. He towered behind Tsu, who was in mid conversation with her cousin.

"Aren't ya gonna introduce us to your friend, Lil' Bits?" William quipped, offsetting his weight by leaning onto the side of the bus. Tsu could see the tension that was overtaking Lily's face. She could tell that the voice sounding behind her, was coming from someone the girl did not like. Tsu rose to a full stance and was determined to be as polite as possible. She knew that the farther south she went, the more direct racism she would most likely encounter, and she didn't want to be the cause of any trouble in her new home-away-from-home. She gracefully turned, daring to face William. He was significantly taller than she was, even in her black and white heels.

"I'm Tsu Monroe and I'm from Connecticut, sir. Nice to meet you," she proclaimed with a smile. She offered her delicate hand in greeting, to the man standing before her. Tsu immediately noticed how dazzlingly handsome the man that hovered over her was. Like one of the golden haired heroes in my story books, she thought to herself. His eyes were like a Caribbean sea and he had the physique of a Greek God. Lean, toned and chiseled to perfection. Tsu tried to appear not to have noticed William's striking features, but he was so beautiful, they were difficult to miss.

A small wave rolled through William's body once he'd gotten a better glimpse of Tsu's, striking face up close. To him, she was stunning! Big, bright, brown doe eyes and reddened full lips on wheaten skin. She's gotta be mine, he thought. Pushing away from the bus, William reached out his lengthy hand and shook her small delicate one firmly.

"I am William Jonathan Baker. Co-owner of Baker and Son's General Store," he responded. He wanted to impress the attractive, petite, colored woman, who captured his gaze.

"Though he's hardly eva there or workin' for dat matta," Lily rudely interrupted.

"Why you lil' devil." William stomped towards Lily, causing her to duck behind Tsu's small frame. Tsu sidestepped quickly, shielding Lily from William Baker's sudden burst of anger. She pressed Lily tightly against her back. And by twisting her body from side to side, she prevented him from getting to her. Tsu was afraid, but she resolved to intercept William's fury, in order to protect her cousin. *Not a hero after all,* Tsu thought to herself.

"Easy, tiger," suggested a gentle, low, voice. Then a hand guided William back to the bus. "Save all that energy for the game tonight, buddy." This man wanted to dismiss the explosive episode off, so he stretched out his own large hand to greet Tsu. "I'm Paul Morrison, this hot head's best friend," Paul explained.

Once it appeared that William was backing off, Tsu took her cautious gaze from him and released one of her hands from Lily's small frame. She reached for the hand now extended before her. When her eyes finally shifted to Paul's face and their hands touched, an electric current shot through both of them, pulsating from head to toe. Paul was noticeably taller than Tsu as well. His eyes appeared cornflower blue, then deep and dark like the night sky. Eyes of a trickster, she considered. He had dark curly brown hair. His jaw line was covered with scruff. He was simplistically beautiful! Not so overwhelmingly attractive, but he had a quiet beauty about him. One that an artist could appreciate.

"Nice to meet you, Sue," he managed to respond.

18

"And you likewise, Mr. Morrison." Tsu quickly withdrew her affected hand. She wasn't quite sure about what had just rippled over and through her body. Or even still, if she were the only one who had felt it. Perhaps she had imagined it.

"Call me Paul, I insist," he said. "And those knuckle heads behind me are Greg Wilks and Randy Mucker." Greg and Randy waved silently in the background, gaping at the poor girl. Tsu smiled politely and gave them a nod. Silence loomed for a few moments longer, as the bus driver continued to empty out all the baggage destined for Lexington onto the parking lot. The driver tipped his hat to Tsu before climbing back onto the bus and pulling out. "Well, it was nice to meet you, Sue. Me and the guys gotta game to get ready for."

"Likewise, sir." She smiled politely. Paul jerked his head back, signaling to his friends that it was time to go. They started back across the road. William walked backwards more collected than he had just displayed, smiling at Tsu the whole way.

"Welcome to Lexington, Sue. Hope to be seeing you around real soon." His eyes were deviant. "Catch you later, Lil' Bits." William winked at Lily once again before he reached Randy's car. Lily glared at him from behind Tsu. They watched as the four of them hopped into the car, and sped off in the direction of the baseball fields.

"Come on, Tsu." Lily grabbed one of her cousin's bags. "Time to head ova ta daddy's butcha shop. He's spectin' us." The two of them headed to the edge of the almost deserted town towards the butcher shop. Her Uncle Jimmy was waiting to take the two girls home for the evening.

~   ~   ~   ~   ~

"Gee whiz fellas! Did y'all see that gal?" Greg inquired.

"That's the best lookin' nigger I've ever seen," Randy stated, driving recklessly down the country roads.

"You mean colored. They don't' like being called niggers anymore," William sarcastically bellowed out.

"I wonder if that's what they all look like in Connecticut. All fancy like," Greg joked. Three of them laughed, but it was mostly Randy and Greg in the front of the vehicle that continued on with their banter. Paul sat quietly in the back seat, flashing a smile every now and again. Mostly he gazed out of the small back window, rubbing his hand, between the crease where he and Tsu had made contact with one another. Paul didn't understand the feeling that had surged through him. He replayed the moment over again in his head when they touched. The way she looked, the soft touch of her skin, the sweet fragrant smell in the air around her. He could barely focus on the conversation taking place in the car. He was trying to understand what he was feeling and what he had felt. There seemed to be something more to her than just the way she looked. But she was colored, so nothing could really come of anything between them.

Beside him, William was also quietly recalling the moment of meeting Tsu. He had a reputation for pursuing colored girls in the county, and quite often got great pleasure in relieving himself with them.

"Fellas, I do believe I have found my next prospect. Y'all know how I likes me a lil' dark meat," William proclaimed, imitating the way the coloreds spoke. Randy and Greg hooted, hollered and cheered him on from the front seat of Randy's car. "She looks a bit more refined than what I'm accustomed to, but with a little finesse, I think I can bring her to her knees." The three of them continued on with their laughter. Paul rode the rest of the trip in silence. He was displeased and bothered with William's proclamation, but he wasn't sure why. Could it have been because he was simply growing tired of William's shenanigans? His outright mistreatment of women, especially colored ones? Or was it something else entirely?

Meanwhile, William conspired next to Paul in the back seat. Sue was exceptional, William thought. He'd have to have her beneath him, like the others.

Chapter Two

It was still vibrantly bright outdoors when Tsu, Lily and Uncle Jimmy arrived at the Gaines' small white home in Green Hill early that night. Green Hill was one of two segregated neighborhoods in the town of Lexington. Although there were a few poorer white families peppered into the community, most of its inhabitants were coloreds. Uncle Jimmy grabbed Tsu's bags and escorted the two young girls up to the charming little house. He was a robust man. He had milk chocolate brown skin, was about 6'5" and he smelled of seasoned meat.

"Ya carryin' rocks in dese bags, Tsu?" Uncle Jimmy asked, climbing up the old front porch steps. Tsu smiled sweetly at him.

"Those are just some of my old books, Uncle James. I couldn't imagine being anywhere in the world without them." The thought of her bags, holding a few of her most treasured possessions, being heavy to such a large man was amusing to her.

"Well, y'ull have pleny o time fo' readin, dat's fo sure. Yur a long way from home Tsu," he commented. "I hope a city gal like you, takes a liken to country livin'." Lily pulled back the screen door, grinning from ear to ear. Tsu followed behind Uncle Jimmy into her new living quarters for the next few months.

~   ~   ~   ~   ~

Dinner was a feast. Suitable for company more deserving than herself, Tsu considered. Aunt Shirley had taken off early from the Beauty Shop where she worked, so that she could prepare this 'Welcome Home' meal for her niece. Tsu was not at all accustomed to the amount of food that her Aunt Shirley had made. Except for during the holidays, Tsu's everyday meals were so much simpler. However, the table was covered with spectacular platters of food. Serving dishes filled with collard greens, chitterlings, potato salad, two fried whole chicken in pieces, biscuits, snapped green beans with potatoes, white rice and for desserts. Pineapple upside down cake, sweet potato pie and peach cobbler.

"On Fridays I usually cooks a big meal on account of I'm at the shop all day long on Saturdays," Aunt Shirley explained. "Go on child, have ya'self a seat and let's get to prayin', so we can get to eatin'," she announced. Shirley waved her hand ushering Tsu to one of the natural pine chairs at the dining table.

Aunt Shirley was awfully well maintained for a woman in her forties. She could easily pass for someone in their late twenties or very early thirties. She had nicely manicured nails, smooth caramel skin and a classic pin up, curly bob. It was apparent that she took great pride in her appearance, as well as her cooking. Tsu thought it was peculiar, that her mother and aunt could be so different from one another. Tsu's mother dressed very conservatively and wore the same hair bun every day of her life. Not to mention that Mother Monroe's cooking couldn't even compare with her sister's food.

"How was the trip, baby? Hope yur lookin' forward ta heat, crickets and baseball," Aunt Shirley suggested with enthusiasm. "This one here," she pointed to her beloved husband. "Thinks he's the modern day Jackie Robinson." Between spoonfuls of food, Tsu laughed. Once she swallowed the bite she had in her mouth, she was able to give her aunt a response.

"It was long and I'm really looking forward to the quiet. Also, I hear baseball is the All American Game, so I suppose there's no time like the present to learn to like it." They all laughed. She had an innocent naivety about her. "This food is so good, Aunt Shirley. My mother doesn't make anything that taste like this."

"Well hell, Anna couldn't make toast if it weren't fo toasters," Aunt Shirley bellowed out. They continued to laugh. "Yur momma was always good at fixin' folks, that's why she became a nurse. Growin' up, us kids did everythin' we could do to keep her out of the kitchen and believe me, everyone's taste buds was grateful fo it."

The meal was the most delicious food Tsu thought she had ever eaten. She wondered how her Aunt had the time to cook the way she did and work at a beauty parlor. Aunt Shirley found the question amusing and explained that she had the mornings to prepare most of the meals before work. Once everything was ready, she would put in all in the icebox and Jimmy or Lily could pop it in the oven to warm it up for the family at dinner time.

"Do ya think that's sumthin you can help out wit as well?" Aunt Shirley asked her.

"Anything I can do to help out, I'd be honored to do. I'm so thankful to you and Uncle James for letting me stay here, and for setting up a place for me to sell my soaps."

"Yur most welcomed, child and call me Uncle Jimmy", he informed her. "I's heard dat soap ya make is somethin' kinda good. Just make sure to give yur aunt and me a few bars on the house and we'll call it even," suggested Uncle Jimmy.

"You've got it Uncle James, I mean, Uncle Jimmy" Tsu replied.

They all sat at the dinner table for some time, telling stories and getting to know each other better. They did their best to eat everything in sight, but it looked like they only tasted a portion of each platter. With the amount of food not eaten, it was evident that there would be plenty of leftovers. At least enough for lunch for the following day, and possibly even dinner. Once all of their bellies were completely stuffed, fatigue began setting in. Aunt Shirley excused the two girls for the night, so that Tsu could get some rest.

Lily escorted Tsu to their room. She was so excited to have Tsu all to herself for a private conversation before bedtime. The two young ladies would not only be spending most of their time together, but they would also be sharing Lily's bedroom during the summer months. Walking Tsu down the short hallway, carrying one of her bags, Lily broke her silence.

"What kinda books did ya bring witcha, Tsu?" Lily was so fantastically curious about her cousin interests. She didn't know many people who made soap, dressed the way Tsu did or who were avid readers.

"Only a few of my most favorite Shakespearian plays," Tsu announced with absolute joy.

"Shake whaaaat?" Lily inquired. She wasn't quite certain of what Tsu had said.

"Shakespeare!" Tsu smiled with gleaming eyes. "He was a famous author from long ago, who wrote some of the most exquisitely wonderful stories," Tsu explained.

"Will ya read me some, sometime?" Lily asked. She put on her most adoring face.

"Absolutely!" Tsu replied following her down the hall. Any excuse or reason to read her favorite plays, was more than alright with Tsu. Even though she had already read each one to the point that should could almost recite them word for word. To her, each time she began to read one again, it was as if she were experiencing it for the first time.

When they arrived at the doorway of the bedroom, the room looked small with the two twin beds jammed into the space. But it was clean and cozy with lightweight white bedspreads to keep them as cool as possible in the summer heat. Tsu didn't mind the close quarters, she was mostly concerned with getting off her aching feet and laying down for a while. It was hotter than she was accustomed to and Tsu had been wearing her high heels for much longer than she anticipated. Lying back on the white spread, she kicked off her shoes one by one, and drifted back to the moment when she and Mr. Morrison shook hands. His chiseled face, that low tempting voice, his rough yet gentle touch. She recalled him requesting that she call him Paul, but she was brought up to use surnames. Also, she took great precautions from being too familiar with any man. *"Some men don't ask."* An interrupting thought from something her mother had told her long ago when she was younger, entered into her mind.

"Whatcha thinkin' bout?" Lily inquired. Her body was stretched out, belly to bed, kicking her wiry legs back and forth on beat. Thankful for the distraction, Tsu thought up a quick response.

"I was just thinking about how hot it is down here."

"Just wait til late July and August. We'll have to night swum most ev'ry night to keep ourselfs cool," Lily proclaimed with excitement in her voice. "I knows a great spot back off in the woods. I'll show ya sumtime." Tsu smiled with enthusiasm. She liked the sound of night swimming. It would be an adventure. But Tsu had more important things on her mind that she wished to discuss with her cousin.

"Lily, what was going on at the bus stop when I arrived? And who were those men?" Tsu's curiosity about the intriguing Mr. Morrison, could no longer contain itself and she wanted to get more information. Even so, she did not want Lily to think that she wanted to know more about Paul. It was preposterous to think that a white man could have a genuine interest in her, or any man for that matter.

"Dat wasn't nuthin at all," she shrugged. "Willy J. Baker likes to try an' get unda my skin s'all. I hear he fancies colored girls and likes tellin' 'em what to do. Sumtimes he gets a bit rough wit 'em. A lot of the men round here can't barely stand 'em for what he's done to some of our girls in Green Hill. But, he's white and we all like his daddy, so there ain't much folks can do. I don't give 'em the satisfaction of lisnen to anythang he says, which gets him so maaaaddd," Lily smiled proudly as Tsu listened to her stories.

"Nobody but me knows that May Jenkins is William's fav'rite colored gal in Green Hill. She's crazy bout him or just plain crazy. Folks say she's a heala and a witch, so they keeps away from her," Lily gossiped. "When those guys drove off earlier this evenin', they were on their way to play their Friday night baseball game. Ya can still hear 'em playin' down there now." Lily pointed out of one of the large bedroom windows. Signaling that somewhere out the white framed panels, there were crowds of people playing and spectating a game. Tsu nodded, indicating to Lily that she could still hear the game in progress. In fact, she had been hearing the commotion faintly in the background since she arrived at the Gaines' house. "Saturdays when us coloreds have our games. I hope you like baseball," Lily concluded.

Tsu propped her head up, pushing her elbow into the bed. "And what about Mr. Morrison, Lily?" Lily smiled. She knew that Tsu had thought that he was as handsome as she did, and that meant they had something in common.

"Paul's Willy J's best frien' since...well always. God knows why," Lily exclaimed. Lily sat up on her bed and looked into Tsu's inquisitive eyes. "I heard dat when Paul was in high school, a colored boy died savin' his life." A big yawn escaped from Lily's mouth and realizing how tired she had become, Lily laid back down on her bed. "Since then, he and his grandmama, before she died dat is, has been mighty fine to color folk in Green Hill," Lily told her with a sleepy expression on her face.

Tsu could tell how tired Lily had become and decided not to push the subject any further. She didn't understand what had taken place earlier between her and Paul Morrison in the street, but she knew that something extraordinary had occurred. Especially since she couldn't stop thinking about him. It wasn't much longer before Tsu's eyes became heavy themselves. Knowing that she would have an extremely busy day tomorrow, Tsu let herself sink into the bed. Tomorrow needed to be spent cleaning out a portion of the old barn in the back, so that she and Lily could make Tsu's soaps there.

~   ~   ~   ~   ~

Back in Connecticut, Tsu had made and sold batches of soap, to a few of the local stores in her home county. She was able to make a good living off of her earnings and it also allowed her the luxury of working in solitude, most days. Tsu was much more comfortable with her nose in a book and her hands in a soap pot than interacting with people. Before she arrived in Lexington, her

29

Uncle Jimmy had arranged for Baker's store to take in shipments of Tsu's soaps, for a small weekly storage fee. Tsu was grateful for the opportunity. She felt that her earnings could help pay her way, while staying at her aunt and uncle's home during her visit. As Tsu's heavy eyes closed for bed, she thought about what kind of adventures she'd undergo during her summer away from home.

~   ~   ~   ~   ~

At the end of the game William, Greg, Randy and Paul headed over to the dugout to retrieve their baseball gear. They proceeded to the spectator stands, where four fine young ladies were waiting for the four of them. A calendar looking red headed woman stepped off of the stands and approached Paul.

"Congrats on your win! That was a good game, darling." She pressed her mouth to his gently. "Shall I accompany you home tonight, Paul?" Megan O'Shea seductively inquired amidst her three friends, Abby, Joy and Carol. Paul's face tensed.

"Not tonight, sweetheart." Paul sounded disinterested. "In fact maybe you shouldn't sleep over for a little while." He was very polite, but still disinterested. "Mrs. Calhoun's been lurking around and I wouldn't want her to get the wrong idea, about the kind of girl you are. You know the woman is the worst kind of gossip there is." He kissed her on the forehead attempting to reassure Megan. "I'll catch up with you tomorrow after my visit with Mr. Hobbs, kay?" Mr. Hobbs was Paul's mentor. Hobbs was a colored man and also resided in Green Hill. Megan was flabbergasted. He had never denied her before, but she respectfully replied.

"If you think that's what's best, darling." Paul smiled at her and then headed over to Randy's car.

"What was that all about, Megan?" Megan's best friend Abby asked, noticing the strange interaction between the two of them.

"I'm not rightly sure," Megan replied with poise, trying not to seem like she was unaffected by her lover's rejection. "He's been acting awfully peculiar, lately."

"Maybe he's just tired. He's been working so hard lately, since the school year ended," Abby offered. She was generally oblivious most of the time, but she tried to help by blurting out some sort of explanation for her friend.

"Or maybe he's thinkin' bout makin' an honest woman out of ya." Joy could no longer contain her silence. "I saw him before the game, coming out of the jewelry store and showing the boys somethin' in a little white box. If I'd have to guess, I bet it was an engagement ring," she blurted out. Megan forcefully took hold of Joy's slim shoulders, desperately wanting Joy's news to be true.

"Oh my goodness, Joy! You tellin' me the truth?" she demanded.

"That's what I saw, Megan. Swear on a stack of Bibles," Joy exclaimed.

"Paul's such a romantic. I bet he proposes under the fireworks Fourth of July," Carol sounded in the background. Paul was

31

always the kind of guy that showed up with flowers, or would pull out a chair, or would do any small gesture to let a girl know that he cared about her. Unlike the rest of his buddies.

"I think you're right, Carol." Megan could sense the jealousy in Carol's statement and she enjoyed being envied as much as she was by the other girls. "Paul's such a stickler for the dramatics, it would have to be during the fireworks." The four ladies scurried off in excitement, making plans for the Fourth of July festivities.

~   ~   ~   ~   ~

Over the course of the next few weeks, Lily and Tsu cleaned out the old barn and set up the front portion of it for their soap making enterprise. The two girls became great friends, as Tsu taught her about the soap making trade. Tsu's willingness to share her beloved books and craft with her cousin, caused Lily to fall more in more in love with her each passing day. Tsu was quite intriguing to her younger cousin, but Lily couldn't understand why Tsu was still single. And at her age.

"How come ya ain't married Tsu? I mean yur so pretty and intrestin'," Lily inquired.

"I was engaged. Over a year ago now to a Mr. Wallace Pinkerton, but it didn't work out." She hesitated, searching for more of an explanation after she noticed Lily's *'tell me more'* face. "I mean, I met his family's approval. Which only meant that I was a light enough shade of brown. And even though I didn't have the pedigree they desired and I have what they referred to as a *'slave name'*. I was educated, so my economic status and my name was overlooked."

"Wat's a slave name?"

"It was a common practice for slave masters to name their slaves after objects or things instead of more traditional or common sounding names, like Mary or John. A Tsunami is something destructive found in nature. A massive wave. Wallace's elitist family frowned upon it, so they called me Sue or they would introduced me as Susan Monroe. I didn't like it very much."

"Well, wat happened? Why aren'cha married?"

"Well although he was very handsome, and everyone thought we made a lovely couple and would make beautiful children," she paused. "Wallace didn't seem to like me at all, in any way, except for having an acceptable look. Not my ideals, career, certainly not my awkwardness with intimacy."

"Wat's dat?" Lily curiously inquired.

"I'll explain it to you some other time." Tsu did not wish to engage in an adult conversation with the youthful girl. Annoyed by Tsu's put off, Lily sucked her teeth.

"So ya ain't married cause he didn't really like ya?" she asked in her most consoling voice.

"Partly. Wallace was also already in love with someone else as well. Ms. Annabelle Cummings, his college sweetheart. She didn't pass his family's paper bag test." Lily's face looked confused by Tsu's statement, so Tsu explained what the test was. "There are colored people who frown upon mixing darker skinned individuals into their families. If someone was darker that a paper bag, they were not viewed as acceptable for marrying into certain families. That's how they are able to breed out the undesired blacker tones. Annabelle's skin was much too dark for his family's liking, and they threatened to withhold his inheritance if he continued his relationship with her. So, after many months of pretending with me, he and Annabelle eventually eloped. It was also rumored that she was carrying his child. Which most likely means that he had be seeing her the entire time, he was with me." Tsu scoffed.

"Were ya mad at him? Wat bout his heritance" Lily questioned.

"I was embarrassed at first. But to tell you the truth, I think I was relieved. And he found out he was going to get his money, whomever he married." Tsu paused. "There wasn't going to be a story book ending with Wallace. At least not for me. Don't fret though. I still feel like I get to be a part of something remarkable with my books, even if not in real life," Tsu responded. The thought of Tsu growing old with books bothered Lily. She believed a man would have to be a fool, not to want to be with someone like her cousin Tsu.

"Just wait til the picnic on the Fourth, Tsu. Someone special's bound ta be there fo ya." Lily assured her. Tsu smiled at Lily and Paul's face immediately came to her mind.

Chapter Three

After three weeks in Lexington, Tsu and Lily were just about to deliver their first batch of assorted scented soaps to Baker's General Store. They began loading up Lily's old red wagon to transport the soaps they had prepared to the store. The day was steaming hot, and both girls had decided that it was best to wait to make the delivery until just before closing time at Baker's. However, it was important to Tsu, to get her product set up and ready for selling before the holiday weekend. She knew that that would be the time when Baker's received most of its local traffic from bus arrivals and departures.

~   ~   ~   ~   ~

Tsu hadn't seen Paul since that first day she arrived in Lexington. Although that hadn't stopped her from remembering his magnificently tricky eyes. His scruffy face or thinking about him every day since she had shaken his hand. She hadn't been interested in a man since her engagement to Wallace Pinkerton ended some fifteen months back. Not that she was really interested in her ex-fiancé in the first place. Wallace initially pursued Tsu because he felt as though she would make a nice adornment on his arm. He couldn't stomach not being the center focus of Tsu's world, as he had been for the many other women in his life he had had the pleasure of knowing.

After his elopement, Tsu was invited to move into her mother's employer's home, Mrs. Ellington, on the south side of town. The accommodations were extremely humbled. Mrs. Monroe and Tsu had put everything they had into Tsu's education. Aside from their wardrobes, which they most often made themselves, they had very simple things. Being away from the scandal and embarrassment of Wallace's marriage, Tsu was determined to make a new start for herself and began making her soaps.

~   ~   ~   ~   ~

It was a long, hot walk from Lily's house in Green Hill to Baker's in the center of town, but Tsu loved it. Breathing in the fresh country air, listening to the rustling of the trees, when if ever the warm wind blew. And the sounds of nature from living in the country. Her imagination was running wild.

"I love the way these grandfather trees frame the road and the way the leaves dangle off of their limbs. This would be the perfect setting for 'A Midsummer Night's Dream', don't you think, Lily?

"I's only understan' yur books when ya splain 'em to me in 'Merican English, so I'll take yur word for it."

"Lily," Tsu muttered. "Make sure you're enunciating all of your words and syllables. Don't forget the beginning or the ending consonant or vowel sounds of all of your words. You are much too intelligent to sound uneducated, my dear Lily of the Valley." Tsu referred to the young girl

"I'm workin' on it. You," she emphasized, "reckon by time ya leave, my talking will be betta?" Tsu paused, sadden by the thought of leaving.

"If you keep practicing every day Lily, it'll get better and better. I promise. Just like the soap making." The idea of it made Lily smile.

Tsu continued to pull the rusty red wagon full with 50 assorted scented bars of soap. Her sandals securely in place between them and the wall of the wagon. She hardly wore any of her pretty dress shoes anymore. She now preferred the blackened soles of her own feet to any stylish shoes. The day was hot and humid and small beads of sweat seeped through her tanning skin. Tsu was thankful for the lightweight, yellow cotton dress she wore. Anything heavier or another color may have made the trip more uncomfortable. Since they waited until the hottest part of the day had come and gone, the air was moving into cooling down as much as it could do for a Virginian July evening.

Lily loved making soap and she loved her cousin Tsu. Everything about her. Lily hoped to be just like her when she finished growing up. She practically imitated everything Tsu did, and followed her everywhere she went. Tsu didn't mind one bit. She was flattered that her little cousin idolized her as much as she did. Tsu thought of Lily as the little sister she never had.

"I love soap makin'! Mixin' the lye, pourin' the molds, addin' the smells...."

"All of those action verbs you've just used, have G's at the end of them. Don't forget to use them." Tsu was amused by Lily

"Dang it." Lily paused, then immediately became excited. "I sounded the G out that time."

"Yes, you did, but dang, is not a word," She told her.

Lily walked and talked beside Tsu all the way to town. She had become quite the little apprentice. With the extra help, Tsu was producing batches of soap much faster than she had ever done so before on her own.

"I'm so excited bout the Fourth of July barbecue this year, Tsu. The solos are gonna be amazin'. May Jenkins is sanging this year for us. Daddy made it so."

"I heard about the 'battle of the solos' from my mother. Seems like a pretty big deal," Tsu responding, pretending to be interested.

"It's only the most impotant event there! It's practically the only time we coloreds get to outshine white folks. If we're better dat is," Lily retorted.

"I see. This May Jenkins must be quite the soulful church singer?"

"Nah, she has a softa sound. The white folk don't think a soulful sound is equal to a classic train voice. So we try an' be like that also."

"Equivalent would be a better word to use rather than equal," Tsu explained. "So what are vocalists singing this year?" Tsu made certain to emphasize the word singing. Lily rolled her eyes in a playful manner before responding.

"Megan O'Shea is singing 'Oh Beautiful' fo the whites and May is sangin' 'My Country Tis of Thee' for us coloreds."

"Oh lord. If it's a competition, why on earth is May singing," she emphasized the G on the word singing for Lily once again, "such a remedial song? For heaven's sake, we sang it in grade school." Tsu was annoyed by the song selection.

"Not rightly sure, but we all knows it and it's easy to play, I suppose."

~   ~   ~   ~   ~

When they finally arrived on Main Street, it was a moderately busy evening for a Friday. It was the weekend before the Fourth of July. Lexington was getting ready for its annual Independence Day picnics in the park by the fields. Tsu and Lily strolled up to the general store and sat themselves down on the steps so that Tsu could put her sandals on her dirty feet, before entering the establishment. Lily did the same, mirroring her cousin's actions. The two of them lifted and carried the wagon up the steps of Baker's. Tsu pulled back the screen door, but before she could enter, she caught a glimpse of Paul a little farther down the road. He was with the three friends she had been introduced to weeks before. But now they were in the company of four sophisticated looking ladies. Paul had his arms wrapped around a pretty, elegant looking red headed woman. Tsu felt her heart drop instantaneously in her chest. Lily, who had already entered the store, walked back to see what had captured Tsu's attention. Without taking her eyes off of Paul and the redheaded beauty he was embracing, Tsu spoke to Lily.

"Who's the redhead Mr. Morrison is holding on to so closely?" Tsu managed to ask the question, losing hope every second Paul held the pin-up lady in his arms. *They look so natural and comfortable with each other*, she perceived and the thought hurt her even further. With a shrug of her boney shoulders Lily replied.

"That's Megan O'Shea. The white's soloist and Paul's sweetheart. Everyone 'spects them to be married real soon, but Paul hasn't axed yet."

Married! At the mere thought of it, tears welled up in Tsu's big brown eyes. The heart that had just fallen out of place was suddenly jolted back into place, and beating fiercely behind her breast. She was caught off guard by the overwhelming flood of emotions. She didn't really expect for anything to happen between her and him. The possibility was absurd. Moreover, why would he want her when he had such a beautiful prize already in his arms?

"What's wrong Tsu? Whatcha bout to cry for?" Lily begged.

"It's nothing." Tsu reined her tears back, and took a deep breath to steady her beating heart. "I just got a little homesick all of a sudden, that's all," Tsu lied. She could offer no other explanation because she barely understood her emotions herself. Saddened by the sight, Tsu simply entered the store to unload her first shipment of soap. Lily hesitated in the doorway, regarding the sight of Paul and Megan. She could sense that Tsu was hurting, and it was from seeing the Paul and Megan embracing. Lily was just beginning to understand sorrow and love the way that Tsu did, due to the story books they read together every single night. Not wanting to make matters worse for Tsu, Lily chose to keep quiet and simply assisted her with the delivery.

~   ~   ~   ~   ~

After the delivery the two ladies skimmed the street as they were leaving Baker's. Paul and the others were nowhere in sight and the town was calmer. Suddenly, Tsu remembered the baseball games every Friday night, in which Lily had told her about. Aware that Tsu's mood had changed, Lily decided to attempt to distract her.

"Fourth of July's gonna be so much fun this year, Tsu. The food, the fireworks, everyone in their red, white or blue," Lily pronounced each word with excitement. "Will ya make me a dress? Like one of your fancy ones?" she asked, her eyes pleading.

"Sure, Lily," Tsu somberly replied. Hearing the sound of her own response, Tsu realized that she sounded and looked absolutely melancholy. She resolved herself and made the choice to pretend to be happier than she actually felt. After all, she had no real justified reason to be upset. "When we get home, no soap for the next two days. We can use a break. And for all of your hard work, I think that you are entitled to a new dress," she uttered.

The two of them started back on their long journey home. They could've went over and waited for Uncle Jimmy at the butcher shop, but it would've been over an hour wait. Besides they liked the walk, even if it was long. Tsu dragged the empty, rusty, red wagon, carelessly throwing her sandals back into it, for the hot walk home. It had taken almost an hour for them to get to the general store from the Gaines' house. Nevertheless, Tsu appreciated having the time on the way back to clear her head. It also helped that Lily diverted her thoughts with ideas about the style and design of the dress Lily wanted Tsu to make for her.

As they walked alongside the road, Tsu and Lily could hear cars speedily approaching from behind them on their way to the baseball fields for the night's game. The fields were much closer to Lily's house than the center of town was. A few last minute traveling cars raced by them, filled with passengers screaming...

"GO BADGERS!"

Paul was in his old black Chevy truck, when he came across Lily and Tsu walking up ahead on the side of the road. Without any thought, he recklessly swerved off the road in front of them, startling the two ladies.

"Can I offer you ladies a ride?" he asked charmingly, stepping out of the driver seat of his truck. His eyes were fixed on Tsu.

"Sure could!" Lily didn't hesitate with her reply. She jumped into the back of his truck with no assistance. Paul smiled at Lily's tenacity, and he picked up the old wagon and placed it into the back with Lily and his toolbox. If Tsu's eyes could've talked. They threw look after look at Lily like, what are you doing? Get out of his truck! Lily pretended not to notice Tsu or her looks. Paul walked over to the passenger's side of his truck and opened the door for the lovely lady.

"Sue?" He motioned for her to get into the truck with his hand and a warm smile. She walked up the side of the truck. She kept her eyes to the ground for fear of what they might've revealed. Paul held out his sizable hand in order to assist her with getting up and into his truck. Tsu accepted it so that she could climb onto the warm vinyl seat. The moment their hands met, there it was again! Heat surging. A current of electricity shooting through the both of them. Tsu quickly glanced up into Paul's concerning eyes. She slipped her hand away slowly, letting the connection linger as their hands parted. Paul, agitated but intrigued, humbly closed the door. What else could he do? He proceeded back to the driver's side of the truck and jumped in.

"Hold on Lily!" he hollered out of his window, as he reignited the ignition. Frustrated by that feeling, he revved the engine and pulled into the road. What is happening to me around her? What could I say to her? Here? Now? How could she look so enticing, glistening with sweat? Paul had not been able to get her off of his mind either, since he laid eyes on her when she first arrived in Lexington. But the touching. The touching made it so much worse.

"So, are you going to the game tonight, Sue?" He stumbled out the first thing he could think of, than immediately felt stupid for asking her that. Why would she be going to the game? It is well know that the coloreds had their own games on Saturday nights and a colored woman would stick out like a sore thumb in a crowd of white faces.

"No. I promised Lily that I'd make her a dress for the Fourth of July picnic Sunday night," she replied through bashful glances. Paul noticed that he was affecting her as well, and he liked it. Maybe she feels something too! He wondered.

"Is that right? You're going to the picnic Sunday night?" he inquired with a hopeful sound in his voice. But suddenly he remembered that the whites and the coloreds would be on separate sections of the park. Running his hand through his loose chocolate curls, he found himself scheming up a way to catch a glimpse of her.

"Well, it seems to be the Lexington thing to do. You know what they say 'When in Rome.'" She shrugged her exposed shoulders, which drew his gaze into her subtle neckline. I can do this, she thought. Be daring for once in your life! "I haven't gotten out very much since I got into town. Are you going, Mr. Morrison?" Her question, desperately seeking a response.

"Yeah, I'll be there. On the white side, but sometimes the fellas and I cross over to the colored side for a good drink or some late night dancing. And you can call me Paul, Sue." He flashed her a quick smile. "Maybe I'll get to see you Sunday night," he blurted out. It would almost be impossible for the two of them to have any kind of interaction. Especially with the fueled tension between the rivals of the soloists.

Does he want to see me? What about the redhead? What could I wear? So many questions and thoughts came to her mind, but the first slipped past her lips before she knew it.

"Would you like to see me Sunday night?" She pinned him with her big doe eyes, challenging him to respond. His face blushed a little at the directness of her question and the boldness of her gaze. He thought, God yes, but he replied much calmer, running his hand across his face.

"I very much would." It was an honest statement, no matter how controlled he was and Tsu felt his sincerity.

"Then I will make every effort to be seen by you, Sunday night." She taunted him with her words. What am I doing? She thought, glancing out of her window.

What is she saying? He thought to himself, feeling hotter from something other than the July heat. He had forgotten that he would be with Megan Sunday night, and how difficult it would be to steal away from her grasp. In the moment, all he could focus on was Tsu. In her yellow cotton dress, her skin moistened by the summer's heat and that smell. God what the hell is that smell? He wondered, filling his nostrils with the scent. Feeling embarrassed by her brash demeanor, she hurriedly change the subject.

"I see you have a tool box and some lumber in the back of your truck. Are you a carpenter?" Appreciating the distraction, Paul responded.

"I do some carpentry work during the summer months. It happens to be a passion of mine, but I'm an English teacher all other times of the year."

Tsu who was a passionate lover of words and books, felt a small fire bloom in her belly. Could he possibly love literature as much as she did? Paul inquired about her occupation and she told him about her soap making venture. Tsu explained to him that she had been a Professor's Assistant in English Literature, almost eighteen months back before her engagement ended.

"You quit teaching because you were getting married?" Paul asked, really wanting to know how or why somebody would've let her get away.

"Not really. Wallace didn't like that I worked. Especially out of the house. *'A woman's place is in the kitchen and in the home,'* he'd use to say. Unfortunately, I'm not very good at being a housewife, which is why I suppose he found himself with somebody else." She sounded so utterly unworthy. Immediately, she regretted letting Paul know that she was a terrible homemaker. What if that is what he's looking for as well? She considered that thought for a moment. Paul observed that Tsu's mood had change. She went from being bold to self-loathing, instantaneously. He couldn't help the urge to rid her from her current sadness.

"Well each of us have our own talents. Seems to me, since you like literature and crafting, that you need to consider the possibility that maybe you're an artist. A creative soul, my gammy would say." He smiled at her. "Anyone can keep a home. It's the visionaries and the artist that make this world interesting." He complimented her bruised ego, in hopes that the girl who had so brazenly propositioned him just moments before would return to him. Tsu smiled at the idea of her being an artist. But his statement made her feel like maybe he could see something extraordinary about her.

"I am no more of an artist than this old truck is a race car, Mr. Morrison." Paul shot her an annoyed look, and she knew it was because she had called him by his surname once again.

"We'll just have to see about that, won't we? And I'll have you know that this old truck is faster than you think." He revved the engine again and pushed the gas pedal to the floor. They zoomed down the road. Lily threw her arms up in the air and cheered as the truck gained speed.

~   ~   ~   ~   ~

They pulled up on the small white house. Tsu found herself cursing how quickly the trip had gone by under her breath. How almost an hour of walking was comparable to a ten to fifteen minute ride by car. Paul exited the driver's side of the truck and scooped the wagon and then Lily out of it.

"Lily, you gaining weight on me? Feels like at least another two lbs.," he teased.

"Very funny, Paul. Someday y'ull see, I'll be just like cousin Tsu." Paul hoped she would be wrong, for all their sakes.

By the time he had gotten to the passenger side of his truck, to let Tsu out, she had already done so herself. So he simply held the open door and took all of her in the only way he could. With his eyes.

"Thanks for giving us a ride," she said politely. "I know you've got a game to get to and I wouldn't want you to be late on our account," she stated. She didn't want him to be worried about getting to the game, or for him to think that it would be her fault if he were late. He chuckled.

"No trouble at all, Ms. Susan Monroe. In fact, it was truly my pleasure to escort such lovely ladies home." He asserted himself to using, what he thought was Tsu's full name. Lily laughed herself right through the front door of her home, which puzzled Paul. Tsu stepped away from him, backing away slowly.

"Susan?" She questioningly repeated. She hated being called Susan. "That's not my name." Embarrassed for assuming the wrong name he simply apologize and asked.

"What's your name then?" A wide and wicked grin came over Tsu's sweet face as she made her way to the front porch.

"Maybe I'll tell you Sunday night. If you can find me that is. I'll have some sort of red on, like dozens of other girls I assume." The screen door smacked against the door jamb as Tsu disappeared into the house. She never looked back as she made her way to the sewing room. She felt as though she had just won some small victory over her male counterpart, like in one of her romance novels.

Stunned and intrigued, Paul was left hanging with no answer, just another taunt. Playful too, I like that. He thought to himself. He climbed back into the driver's side of his truck, backed out of the driveway and headed to his game. He'd have to find her Sunday night. She had just about dared him to, and Paul Morrison never backed away from a dare.

"Red. Of course a red dress," he said aloud to himself. Everyone in town would be wearing red, white and/or blue. But the majority of the women mostly always chose red. And how was he going to be with her there, without the community becoming aware of his intentions? To become better acquainted with this colored girl. Paul pulled into the field just in time to hear...

"PLAY BALL!"

Chapter Four

It was just about dusk and Tsu was putting the final touches on Lily's dress. Aunt Shirley had forbidden Lily from wearing a red dress because of her age. Shirley did not want to give any of the young men the wrong impression about her daughter, so Lily had to settle with a blue dress. Tsu inherited her white evening dress from her mother and once on, it would be figure flattering. Lily regarded her figure and compared it to her cousin's. Tsu's adult body was more developed than Lily's, but Lily knew that her womanly curves would be soon on their way.

"Mama, I feel like a princess. I really enjoy being girly sometimes." Lily said to her mother.

"Well, it could happen more of'en if ya let me dress ya and style yur hair more," Aunt Shirley lovingly answered. Tsu finished the last stitches on Lily's dress.

"That reminds me of a song from this musical I saw on Broadway a few years back about girl, who REALLY enjoyed being a girl," Tsu intervened.

"Can you teach it to me or sang it, pleeeeease, Tsu?" Lily begged. Tsu looked around as if she was deliberating over Lily's request. Without warning, she began singing and acting out the Flower Drum Song, 'I Enjoy Being a Girl'.

~   ~   ~   ~   ~

As she finished singing, Tsu grabbed Lily and they both fell to the couch in laughter. Uncle Jimmy entered the room annoyed. He was not amused by all the time it was taking the three of them to get dressed.

"Dat's real nice Tsu, but can you gals hurry up and get ready?" He looked to his wife and perceived that she hadn't even changed out of her church clothes yet. "Shirley! Yur not even close to ready. Ya knows I gotta perform t'night and I's worried bout May."

"Hush, Jimmy. Beauty takes time. And if yur so worried bout that girl, ya shouldn't pushed fo her to be the singa."

"Not dis again." Jimmy gave her a stern look. Aunt Shirley was habitually late, but she knew that tonight was important to her husband and she didn't want to get into an argument. The three ladies dispersed to their quarters to finish readying themselves for the party.

~   ~   ~   ~   ~

Tsu looked at her reflection in the mirror and began taking out her curlers. She pinned a red flower into her hair. To compliment herself, she whispered.

"Thanks momma. Like a jewel on an Ethiope's ear, I hope." Some exquisite line from a Shakespearian tragedy she adored, where Romeo describes Juliet's beauty. But more than beautiful she felt... could she dare think it, desirable? Tsu had never thought of herself as desirable before, but she wanted to be and she wanted to be so

51

for Paul. Sexiness had always eluded her, because she felt such a discomfort with her own body. Not to mention, the female characters she revered from her books were never bestowed with sexiness. Beauty no doubt, but sex appeal was as foreign to them as it had been to her.

~   ~   ~   ~   ~

The two baseball fields were lit up marvelously with strung lanterns on both sides of the park. Both whites and coloreds were enjoying the night on their separate sides of the fields, with very minimal intermingling occurring.

Megan O'Shea, wearing a red dress that flared at the waist, clung to Paul's side all night. She was absolutely expecting that tonight was the night that Paul would ask her to marry him. She signaled to her girlfriends to accompany her over to the punch table. Paul was thankful for the break. She had been underneath him for most of the festivities.

"This has got to be the night," she whispered to Abby.

"What could be more romantic than a proposal just before the fireworks, Megan?" Abby posed wistfully.

"I've already given myself to Paul, on multiple occasions. Let me tell you, that man knows how to make love to a woman" She traced her fingers down the side of her arm, as she recalled their last interlude. She let out a deep breath. "There's nothing left but marriage for us."

"Oh Megan." Abby was embarrassed by Megan's bold statements. The girls broke away from the punch table, as it was becoming crowded. They didn't want for anyone to overhear them speaking.

"We can't all be saints like you, Abby. But you've already got your ring from William. Surely you don't think that Paul was my first? At our age?" Megan scoffed at her ignorant and innocent friend. "Newsflash he wasn't a virgin either. Fortunately for me, some other woman had already trained him and trained him well," she admonished. "And we all know that William of yours is not the purest fella either." Abby was embarrassed by Megan's harsh words, as she lowered her eyes to the ground. She only wanted to believe the best of William, no matter what others tried to tell her about him. Carol and Joy tried to cover up their laughter.

"You could have anyone you want in all the counties in Virginia, surely Paul knows that," Joy added.

"You would think, but he's been acting more strange than usual. Not talking 'bout all that lovey dovey crap his grandmother filled his head with growing up." Megan began contemplating Paul's recent demeanor, as she regarded him with her friends.

"I'm certain tonight's the night, Megan," Carol assured her, despondently.

"It better be. After I claim my win in the solos and the fireworks commence, I'm gonna claim Paul Morrison. Til death us do part." All the ladies laughed, as they rejoin their men out on the field.

Megan already presumed that she and Paul would have been married by now, or at the very least, engaged. There was no better catch in the county than Megan O'Shea. The beauty who stood to inherit a small fortune from her daddy's coal refineries. She stood slender and tall, pale-freckled kissed skin, chestnut brown eyes and perfectly proportioned lovely features on her oval face. She had all the attributes of a Hollywood starlet. There was no question that Megan was a catch. It perplexed everyone in town, why the small town teacher had been hesitating to propose marriage to the very appealing Ms. O'Shea. Though, even if she could have anyone else in town, she only wanted Paul. All of her friends were in agreement. The Fourth of July picnic would be the most romantic time for him to ask, especially after she won her solo.

~   ~   ~   ~   ~

Paul had indulged Megan most of the night, but anticipated another moment when he could break free from her grasp. Amongst the chatter of the four ladies, he heard them inquire about Megan's readiness to represent them this year in the solos.

"You think Megan's ready for her solo, Paul?" Abby nudged Paul in the direction of her friend.

"She looks amazin' tonight, don't you think?" Joy chimed in. Looking into Megan's eyes, Paul wiped his hands down his smooth face. It appeared that he had had other things on his mind.

"I think she will be amazing tonight, as expected." His statement had very little emotion.

"She should. Daddy spares no expense." Carol whispered to Randy. They both laughed to themselves.

Paul had forgotten that Megan would be singing the solo for them. That's the perfect time, he thought. He could easily sneak away during the solos and catch back up with Megan and the gang, before they all went for their customary late night swim at the creek. This would be his only opportunity to see Tsu.

~   ~   ~   ~   ~

Tsu commanded everyone's attention when she arrived at the picnic. She was a vision in her figure flattering white dress, belted at her waist with a red sash. Although it was a bit old fashioned, having belonged to her mother, none seemed to complain. She was uneasy with her oozing sensuality and all the attention it was attracting. Most of the color folk in Green Hill didn't really know Tsu very well, since she didn't come out to much more than the occasional Saturday game. But the men sure wanted to find out, as they proceeded to approach her. They were quickly redirected when Big Jimmy Gaines stepped forth. His arms were crossed and his face was stern.

"She's not fo' you, fellas. Y'all best be on yur way." Uncle Jimmy explained with a serious expression on his face. Out of the corner of his eye, a commotion near the stage caught his attention.

He went to investigate the disturbance. Not a soul approached Tsu in his absence, but the eyes she held captive spoke volumes. The men with their long lustful gazes and the women glared at her with disgust and jealousy. Tsu hadn't the time or care to be concerned with any of their looks. In haste, she skimmed the sea of the multiple shades of brown faces, looking for only one white one, Paul's. But he was nowhere in sight. Suddenly, Uncle Jimmy returned to Tsu's side in a panic.

"Tsu, we gotta real problem here," he expelled. "May Jenkins, t'night's soloist, has gott'n herself so drunk, dat she's passed out at home plate and she can't sang," Uncle Jimmy explained. "Now your momma told us pleny o times that you had a good voice, Tsu."

"Uncle Jimmy, you know I'm uncomfortable around people, especially large groups. I don't think I can...."

"Com'on Tsu? I just saw ya sangin' in the house not more than a hour ago."

"That was different, Uncle Jimmy. That was for Lily and at home." Tsu was nervous. She didn't like being the center of attention.

"Now Tsu, we needja. I wouldn't ax if it weren't impotant. White folks beat on us all year. All the time Tsu. This is one of the onliest ways we gets to show 'em that we can be betta than them. Dat we got sumthin' good in us, they can't take away. Com' on, Tsu. Do ya know the song?"

"Of course I know it, Uncle Jimmy. But I'm not singing that juvenile song."

"Whatcha wanna sang then? Anythang!" Tsu thought for a moment, then she replied.

"I can sing '*Tis A Gift*'." She shrugged in disbelief. She couldn't believe what she was agreeing to.

"We don't know dat song. Y'ull have to sang it all by yurself, wit no music behind ya?"

"Of course I will," she hopelessly sounded.

"Thanks so much, Tsu. Much appreciated." He hugged her. "Now just do the best ya can do. We're not forfeiting to those bastards today. A battle fair and square." Uncle Jimmy scurried back over to the stage to let his band mates know the good news.

Tsu had been told stories from her mother about the Independence Day picnics and how important the solos were. Mostly because of the unspoken competition between the whites and the coloreds. Even though a winner would not be announced, it was understood by both sides that year after year they were competing for which side sang best during the festivities. She remembered what Lily had told her. That a heavily soulful sound would not be considered equivalent to a traditionally trained voice. She was also worried that the song that she chose, didn't mention anything about America. However, it was about freedom, which was the backbone of the United States of America's core values and the very thing coloreds had been striving for.

~   ~   ~   ~   ~

"I do love when you clean yourself up." Megan pushed herself up onto her toes to meet Paul's clean shaven face. "How bout a kiss for good luck, darling?" she insisted. Paul met her request with his mouth pressed sweetly to hers. When their lips parted, Megan walked away towards the stage in order to prepare for her singing debut. Paul escorted William, Greg and Randy, in the opposite direction. Steering them over to the colored side of the field. This would give him most likely his only chance to find or at the very least, see Tsu again.

"Hey fellas, whatta ya say bout going over to Boomer and getting some moonshine?" Paul asked.

"Sounds like you were readin' my fucking mind," Randy commented.

"Yeah, if I get one more old lady offerin' me an ice tea, Joy may become a widow," Greg joked.

"That may not be a bad thing for Joy," William boasted and the three other friends laughed.

"Thanks a lot, William. Yur so funny, I forgot to laugh." Greg was accustomed to being the butt of William's jokes.

"Awww, don't be mad, Greg. Tell ya what, you can have the first glass. We wouldn't want you to end your life now, would we? Besides, I can use a real drink. I'm almost outta beer." William took a swig from his bottle.

~　　~　　~　　~　　~

Back near the stage the three ladies were primping Megan before her performance. Carol caught sight of the four men heading to the colored side of the fields.

"Where do you think they're going?" Carol asked the girls, watching them walk away from the white side of the festival.

"Maybe it's to go get the ring," Abby responded with excitement. Carol rolled her eyes.

"Cross your fingers girls. In the next fifteen minutes, I'm gonna be the future Mrs. Paul Isaac Morrison." Megan could not contain her own excitement.

~   ~   ~   ~   ~

The four men were able to grab a few quarter filled glass jars of moonshine that Boomer Wilson had concocted. Megan expectantly, was singing her solo flawlessly. There was no doubt. Megan was the best the county had to offer, in just about every way. Paul looked around eagerly, trying his hardest to be inconspicuous, but he could not locate Tsu.

"Time to go boys, Allons-y," he said in French. "One glass is more than enough of this shit," William explained. Several of the colored men were hatefully eyeing William down. If only they could get him back for all that he had done to a few of their young women. William only smirked at them. He knew there was nothing these disadvantaged colored men could do to him. However, he was wise enough to know not to linger in their presence or on their turf for too long.

Paul hadn't found Tsu yet, so wasn't ready to leave, but William was already steering the others back over to their side. Just as soon as Megan finished singing her solo, Jimmy announced on the small wooden stage, that his niece, Tsu Monroe would be singing 'Tis a Gift.' The four friends turned, when they heard Tsu's name being announced. They remembered being introduced to a colored Sue weeks before. Could this have been her? Before a sound even came out of her exquisite red mouth, Paul caught her in his sights. Her voluptuous figure in white. A surge of heat ran through his body landing in his groin.

"Wait! Is that my girl?" William stammered out, gulping down his drink. He had been working diligently on how drunk he could get before the end of the night. Wounded and offended by his friend's statement, Paul's face tensed and the heat that was in his groin quickly relocated to his fists.

That's my girl, Paul thought. She's dressed for me and here for me. Abruptly, reality kicked in and Paul remembered that Tsu was neither William's nor his. That in fact, he was with Megan and William would be marrying Abby Ridley next month. Although that hadn't stopped William from indulging himself with other girls from time to time.

"She looks incredible, Willy J. But I thought the Jenkins witch was supposed to be sangin' for the coloreds?" Randy inquired.

"Maybe one of her own spells backfired and she turned herself into a toad or somethin'," Greg made a bad joke at May's expense. William cut his eyes in Greg's direction in such a way, that Greg knew to silence himself. It was strange to him that May wasn't there. However, Tsu was the new prize in his eyes.

"Who knows what happen to May, but let's see what our new found friend Sue has to offer us here," William commented.

Tsu with closed eyes, inhaled deeply and began to sing.

Tis a gift to be simple. Tis a gift to be free
Tis a gift to know just where we ought to be

All eyes and ears paid tribute to her. It was unexpected that a colored, could sing so angelically. Paul was in awe and thought it to be one of the sweetest sounds that he had ever heard. He wanted to close his eyes in order to experience the sound more intensely, but he couldn't take his gluttonous eyes off of her.

And when we find ourselves in the place just right
T'will be in the valley of love and delight

"Holy shit! Megan's gonna be shitting bricks over this," Randy snickered. Paul paid no mind to anything other than Tsu.

Once true simplicity is gained,
to bow and to bend one shan't be ashamed

To turn, turn, will be our delight
Til by turning and turning we turn round right

~   ~   ~   ~   ~

Back on the white side of the field, Megan was outraged.

"This is not happening right now. This is supposed to be my night." She gestured with a dismissive hand to the girls. "Someone go and fetch me something hard to drink. And where the hell is Paul?" Joy scurried off to find Megan's date and a drink.

~   ~   ~   ~   ~

William took a swig from his glass, as he adjusted his crotch. It was as if some sort of irritation had occurred. One did and had been occurring since Tsu stepped off that bus three weeks prior. William tried indulging himself with Abby, who was insistent on waiting until they were married to become intimate. So he found himself in whorehouses and with a few of the girls he frequented. None had satisfied the craving he had developed over the last few weeks. Not even May Jenkins, who had been his confidential yet favorite past time.

"I need to have Sue, especially seeing the way she looks in that white fucking dress," William proclaimed under his breath.

Once true simplicity is gained,

62

to bow and to bend one shan't be ashamed

To turn, turn, will be our delight

Til by turning and turning we turn round right

"Come on boys," Randy called out. "We'd best get back to soothe over the County Queen at her obvious defeat in the solos." He laughed as they headed back just as Tsu's solo was coming to an end. Paul was staggering behind. He needed to get her attention.

Tsu inhaled deeply as the last note escaped from her slender throat. When she opened her thankful eyes, it was to cheers and applause. Aunt Shirley and Uncle Jimmy looked on their niece, so pleased and proud by her performance and for the message it conveyed. She felt good that she had done something important for Green Hill, something that they could be hold their heads up high for.

Tsu spied Paul off in the distance. He was walking away backwards, heading back to the other side of the fields. He gave her the slightest wave with his hand hooked around his belt loop. He hoped she had seen it. With her hands at her sides, she gave him a quick wave back. Paul pointed to the field house, held up his right hand and mouthed the words "five minutes". Tsu redirected her sight on the small building Paul had pointed to, and carefully nodded without drawing any attention to the secret conversation between the two of them. It reassured him that she had understood that he wanted her to meet him there. She worked her way through the crowd of people to get herself a glass jar of water. After a few more minutes of uncomfortable praise, the Green Hill community eventually turned their attentions back to the festival and the lighting ceremony that was about to launch.

~   ~   ~   ~   ~

Paul allowed his friends get a few yards in front of him before he veered off, heading over to the field house. But before the other three men completely crossed the field, William spotted his friend splitting off and decided to follow after him to see what he was up to.

~   ~   ~   ~   ~

When the fireworks began when Paul arrived, but Tsu hadn't made it to the back of the field house yet. Paul looked up above him, as explosive lights and colors flashed and illuminated the night sky. He didn't quite understand what he was doing, but he knew he needed to be there and with her. Tsu stealthily crept up on him, as he was distracted by spectacle of the fire in the sky. Reaching out for him, she took hold of his hand in hers. Paul didn't say a word to her. Entranced in this perfect moment, he only stroked the side of her cherry wood skin with his free hand. His thumb caressed the palm of the hand he was holding. They gazed deeply into each other's eyes. Magnificent lights exploded above them, banging in the air of the night, but they took no notice. Paul raised her chin up to him, lowering his own in the process and placed his mouth on her full, red lips. It was as if the fireworks were inside of them, and not bursting above their bodies. Paul felt the blood rebuilding in his groin, as he lifted and backed Tsu up against the field house wall. He pressed his strong body firmly against hers, sandwiching her between him and the wall. He kissed her passionately with want, on her mouth and across her neckline. They had both forgotten themselves, their places and had become reckless in their pursuit for one another. Paul hadn't been consumed with such need for a woman in a long while, but never a colored woman. Though he had seen plenty he thought were attractive, something about Tsu exceeded the color of her skin. She became the object of his new found desire. Paul feared he would not be able to walk away from this situation, nor would he want to. He grasped one of her breast as he continued to work her neckline. The contact alarmed her.

"Easy," Tsu breathed into his ear, trying to subdue the passion that was building inside of her own belly. She could feel his erection against her torso, and became fearful that he was going to take her right there on the back of the field house. His intentions seemed pretty clear to her what he wanted to do. "I can't do this," she whispered, hopeful, but uncertain if he would stop. Paul removed his lips from her neck. He inhaled and exhaled sharply, trying to regain control of the ravenous objective that had come over him. He tenderly kissed the side of her warm face, gently lowered her body back on the ground and pulled his body apart from hers.

"I know," he sighed, overwrought with his own emotional state and his erection. "I'm sorry, I didn't mean to get so carried away." It was tremendously difficult for him to put any kind of distance between the two of them. "I thought you said that you would be wearing a red dress tonight." He tried to distract himself.

"I said nothing of the sort." She laughed. "I said, that I would have some sort of red on." She pointed to the flower in her hair and caressed her lips where after the kissing him, only a faint shade of lipstick could be made out. Lastly, she pointed to her red belt. "I assumed white would be easier for you to find me in, amongst all the red dresses." Paul smirked and regarded the contrast of her tanned skin to the powder white fitted dress. She was completely appealing to him. Not only in looks but also with her playful wit.

"Sue, tell me your name?" he begged, trying to concentrate on anything other than the sexual tension coursing between them. She smiled at him, remembering the game she had made of it just days before. Sliding away from him she muttered.

"Next time. I promise." She fixed herself as best she could before disappearing around the side of the field house. Paul waited out the predicament he now found himself in for a few moments more. Once his exhilarated state had subsided enough for him to rejoin his group, he took off in the opposite direction from Tsu. He knew that Megan and his friends would be looking for him. Conveniently, he could tell them he was with Mr. Hobbs and none would question it.

William stepped out of the darkness of the tree line, taking the last swig of his drink. He tossed the glass jar aside, as anger pulsated through his face. He'd gotten quite an eyeful of Tsu and his best friend.

"This is how it's gonna be?" he gritted through his teeth. "He knew she was mine!"

Chapter Five

Not long after the fireworks were over, William and the rest of the group met at the creek for their customary Fourth of July swim and bonfire. This was the usual routine, for the young folk in town after the fireworks. Megan was utterly distraught over being defeated in the solos, and the apparent affirmation that Paul was not going to ask her to marry him tonight. She consumed beer after beer, as she sat near the bonfire adjacent to an inattentive Paul.

"Your solo was much better, honest Megan." Abby was lying, but she wanted to console her beloved friend.

"Your voice is much more sophisticated than that colored's voice," Joy chimed in.

"Come on girls, there's no need to lie to her," Randy crudely informed them.

"Yeah, that nigger sang better," Greg added. "She looked better too," Greg whispered in Randy's direction. He and Randy laughed.

"Greg!" Joy shouted, outraged that they could suggest a thing, and in front of Megan.

"This year they were just plum better. I'm sorry if that hurts your feelings, Megan." Randy wasn't sorry. He didn't care about her feelings one way or another. And since Paul didn't seem to be paying any attention to them telling her like it was, Randy didn't mind giving it to her straight.

On the bank of the creek, the party of people maintained the bon fire and drank while others cooled off in the water. William and Paul were unusually quiet, both distracted by their own inner turmoil, but their friends were too intoxicated and immersed in their good time to notice. It didn't take long for Megan to become inebriated. Paul was growing increasingly annoyed with her, in more ways than one. She was an avid party girl and he didn't appreciate how drunk she would allow herself become. He felt it was unbecoming of a woman to get as intoxicated and out of control as she would do. Often he have to carry her unconscious body home and deal with the repercussions of her drunkenness the following morning.

~   ~   ~   ~   ~

Down the creek from the bonfire, there was a small cliff called Hawk's Ledge, with a rope swing hanging from a giant tree limb. Two bodies were faintly spotted by Greg, peering over the ledge in the midnight air.

"Holy Shit, Megan! I think that's that colored gal who out sang you earlier wit Lil' Bits." Greg teased and mocked her with his laughter. Megan's ego, was bruised by his comment. She became incredibly vexed with him, but she was too drunk to stand up to give Greg a piece of her mind. When she tried to, she doubled over and vomited into the sand. She fell to her knees, then onto her back, nearly passing out in her own puke.

"A swing and a miss, ladies and gentlemen," Randy drunkenly cried out, referring to Megan's failed attempt to best Greg. Paul knelt down beside her and relocated her flaccid body away from her vomit and closer to the warmth of the fire.

"Sleep it off Megan. You most likely won't feel any better tomorrow." He was all too familiar with how crabby and cranky she could be the next day, hung-over.

Paul and William discreetly watched Tsu and Lily's faint bodies from up creek. William kept a watchful eye on his buddy as well, but Paul's stare barely faltered, as he shielded his gaze from his companions. His only thoughts were on how he could get down there to Sue.

Fortunately, the night was winding down and the creek began clearing out from most of the late night swimmers. The four couples were the last remaining bodies left. Abby, Joy and Carol had decided they were ready to go home as well. They packed up their things and made their way to their cars parked up the hill. Paul seized an opportunity to send Megan home with Greg and Joy.

"Joy, take Megan home with you, will ya? I wanna go back and break things down at the fields and get an early start for the morning. She'll have a hangover for sure and will need some tending to tomorrow." Joy nodded in agreement, she absolutely adored Megan. Paul carried her unwilling body to Greg's car and sent them on their way. Once he had heard the cars pull off, Paul put out what was left of the bonfire and jogged down the wooded edge of the bank. He knew that there was Rope Bridge that connected to the

70

other side of the creek, just pass the cliff. Once he had gotten across, he merely needed to work his way up the hillside, to Hawk's Ledge. It was nearing midnight and he was thankful that Tsu and Lily had not retired for the evening yet.

~   ~   ~   ~   ~

Paul walked up on the two of them quietly. He observed them for a few moments. Tsu sat on a stretched out crocheted blanket, which Lily had also sprawled her body upon. Tsu began braiding her hair into two cornrows, besides Lily's worn out body. Finishing her braids, she pulled her knees into her chest and begun staring up into the starlit sky.

"Hey Lily." Paul walked out of the woods wiping his nervous palms on his thighs. Lily was exhausted by the night's events and her quick dip in the creek. She murmured out something so incoherent, that neither Paul nor Tsu could make out what she was saying. They laughed as Lily wrapped herself up tighter in the blanket.

"Hey." He directed his next greeting at Tsu, as he took a seat on the other side of Lily's dampened body. He sat with bent knees smiling at her, trying to think up some way to spark up a conversation with her.

"Hello, Mr. Morrison," she replied. Even though he already requested several times that she use his first name. She was certain that by doing this, it would engage him into a discussion. Paul cocked his head back and his loose curls fell away from his face.

"I've told you a few times now, it's Paul. Unless I'm in the classroom, please call me Paul," he pleaded. He leaned in, closer over Lily's body finding Tsu's ear. "Besides, I think at this point we've been familiar enough with each other for us to use our first names." He voiced, softly placing a gentle kiss on her exposed shoulder. Paul had a fetish for shoulders and necklines. He thought they were the most enticing part of a women's body. One in which he liked to pay careful attention too. Tsu blushed at his directness. "Wanna go for a swim?" His eyes lit up at the thought of her in the water and in his arms. This time, without that dress. It was absolutely appealing, but he imagined that what was underneath it, would be that much more alluring.

"Sure! I've just finished my braids," she replied. He quickly helped her up to her feet. Tsu was also keen on being in his arms and kissing him again. But she was so afraid that he would want more than what she was willing to do. She wondered if he would be less likely to exhibit the control he had displayed earlier on the field house. It had been well over a year since she had been with a man. When her engagement ended, she became even more insecure with herself, sexually. She knew that Wallace found her to be disappointing in bed, as he would let her know how unsatisfied he was after his release. Telling her that she was as much fun as a sack and thanking God that she was at least attractive.

The sparks that ignited within her with Paul, were much different than anything she'd ever felt before. However, with only her past experiences to rely on, she ultimately believed that she would not be able to satisfy Paul either.

~   ~   ~   ~   ~

Paul stripped off his shorts and shirt, revealing his trim and toned torso and cotton white boxer shorts. She could faintly see scaring on his right shoulder. He watched as Tsu apprehensively slide the white dress and her slip to her ankles. She stood before him clothed in black under garments. Paul let out a sigh at the sight of her sculpted petite frame. He extended his hand to her.

"Trust me," he requested, escorting her over to the edge of the cliff. "It's just to cool off for a bit." He brought her to the edge. "Now you've gotta make sure to jump far enough out because there's a ledge down there you can't see. With jagged rocks. I don't want you to get hurt." Tsu was well aware of the ledge. She had been swimming here for weeks now with Lily, but she nodded in agreement with a half-smile on her face. She appreciated that he was being protective of her. It was an endearing quality. "Come on?" He led her a few yards away from the edge. Holding hands, they both ran and jumped off the cliff, into the dark creek. It was instantly cooling. They eased closer and closer to the bank, until they could just about touch its gritty bottom.

The temped water was a refreshing delight from the heat. They waded and circled about one another, without getting too close. Paul could sense her apprehensiveness about being there, alone with him. He thought it best not to advance upon her. He would let her make the first move this time, if she wanted to. He hadn't expected to feel so excited by someone. It was invigorating to be so. He was starting to believe that the stories his grandmother had told him weren't real, and was just about to give up on the possibility of finding somebody like Tsu.

"You've shaved your beard. Was it for the barbeque?" she inquired.

"I did. I figured I didn't have to look like a slob every day. I do clean up nice, don'tcha think?

"I suppose. But I think I prefer you with facial hair. There's something very attractive about how it looks on you," she admitted, somewhat embarrassed.

"Well now. I'll never shave again, if it pleases you." Tsu smiled as she continued to wade in the water.

"Well, I wouldn't say never. I wouldn't want you to start looking like the mountain men in the hills now. But the shadow definitely has its appeal." They both laughed as they waded closer to the shore, crouching in the creek as they continued to talk.

"So....it's officially next time," he announced. He dipped his head back into the water, forcing his hair to slick back off of his face. "Are you going to tell me your name Sue?"

Tsu hesitated for a moment and a devilish grin crept onto her face. She toyed with the thought of withholding her name for a bit longer, but ultimately decided that he was right. It was next time and she had promised.

"My name is Tsunami," she offered.

"Su-na-me?" He repeated phonetically, unsure if he had heard her correctly.

"T-S-U-N-A-M-I." She spelled it out. "Like the natural disaster," she explained.

"Tsunami, huh?" He let the name play off of his tongue. "Tsunami." He liked the way the sound of it rolled off of his lips. "How'd you get a name like that? Tsunami," he sounded once again.

"My father was stationed on a naval ship off the coast of some Hawaiian islands just before the war when a mild Tsunami hit the islands damaging some of the local villages. I was born eight days later, in Connecticut, under complicated conditions. My mother would never be able to have another child, so my father decided that my name should be Tsunami. A destructive wave on the Earth's surface." She felt insignificant just thinking of the meaning of the word, and how her father must've felt about her. "I just go by Tsu though."

Paul saw the angst on her disquieted face and wanted to rid the lovely Tsunami of any feelings of irrelevance.

"Some people consider natural disasters to be a way the Earth cleanses itself. After the Tempest all things are made anew." Tsu thought to herself, if he were making a reference to Shakespeare's 'The Tempest'. He was an English teacher after all. Surely he would be familiar with Shakespeare's work.

"That's an interesting story though. I'm named after my grandfather, on my mother's side." He chuckled and she laughed, letting some of her uneasiness melt away. He began to enjoy the way her laugh sounded, as he observed her closely in the water.

Paul, under the impression that she had become more relaxed with him, waded closer in her direction because he needed to be nearer to her. When Tsu did not retreat or protest to his advancement, he continued to move towards her. Once they were face to face, he glided his hand over her head, smoothing back her braids. He had never touched a colored girl like this before. She gleamed in the moonlight amidst the shimmering dark water. He stroked the side of her damp cheek with the back of his hand. He was touching her more delicately than any man had ever done so before.

"You're so beautiful, Tsunami," he told her, sliding his hands down her slim shoulders.

"It's just the heat and this setting and please....call me Tsu, Mr. Morrison." He laughed as his eyes took more of her in.

"It's much more than that. Since the first time I saw you, Tsunami, I've thought that you were the most beautiful thing I had ever seen." He ran the back of his hand down the side of her drying cheek, once again. She examined him as he carried on with his confession. "I haven't been able to get you out of my mind since the moment we touched, the first day you arrived in Lexington," Paul admitted. "Something extraordinary happened to me when I touched you. Do you remember that day?"

"Yes, I do, and I've thought about you too since then, but then I saw you with that redhead in town and..." Tsu didn't finish her sentence. She wondered if he would try to mislead her in some way, so she left her statement hanging, to see how he would respond to it.

Paul was caught off guard by her report and he waded back trying to understand the situation better himself. He wasn't thinking about Megan O'Shea, even if everyone else thought that he should marry her. How could he consider marrying her now? Now that he had found Tsu? How could he, when all he wanted was the impossible? A colored girl. His hometown nor his friends would ever permit him to be with her openly, due to the color of her skin. He followed up to her unfinished statement as honestly as he could.

"The red head's name is Megan and she is my longtime girlfriend and we are expected to get married, I suppose at some point." He inhaled deeply. "But I swear to you," he smiled. "That since I met you, I find myself coming up with reasons and ways to be around you. I have no idea what I'm doing or why I am so compelled to do it, but I can't stop thinking about you or wanting to be with you." His face tensed as he struggled to find a reason. "Megan is someone that looks right but in other ways, just isn't. You're an unexpected, but much appreciated surprise for me, Tsunami." His explanation was desperate and so forthcoming, if it were indeed true. Still, she had understood what he meant. She herself had been presumed to be a good fit for Wallace because of how they looked together. In actuality they couldn't have been more wrong for each other. Tsu wasn't quite sure what, if anything, she meant to Paul though. It felt and sounded like there was a possibility that she could've mattered to him, but not as much was divulged.

Hearing his own reasoning out loud, Paul realized how absurd he sounded and feared the worse. He fully expected Tsu to march herself out of the water, onto the bank and to walk right out of his life forever. He felt that the response he had given her was lame, but he didn't want to lie to her about who Megan really was to him.

Tsu could see the internal struggle that Paul was having, as his facial expressions suggested as much. She knew that he didn't understand it any more than she did, and in the moment she didn't care. She only wanted to be closer to him and to ease his distress. She could no longer bear the distance between them. Tsu reached out for him, wrapping her hands behind his neck. She pulled herself onto his lap, encircling her legs around his core, until their noses were touching. She had never been this bold in all her life, but she was acting on impulses caused by him.

He placed his hands on her small back holding her securely to his body. He hadn't felt in all his life as complete as he did now, before this moment. Now here with Tsu, he felt a wholeness he had been yearning for. Paul was relieved, as he nuzzled his nose against hers. Cradling his hand at the base of her head, he took her mouth into his slowly and sensually. He did not want to rush this kiss as he had done so earlier in the evening, with their first kiss. He also did not want Tsu to think that he was pressuring her in any way to do more, though he was willing to explore her further. She held him close to her as well, running her hands through his wet and whirly hair. It was so easy and comfortable to be with him. Her pelvis innately sank deeper into his lap and she could feel him rising beneath her bottom. Not wanting to give him any ideas that things would progress with them, she gently pushed her body away and off of his.

"I'd better go," she said. Paul had dreaded hearing those words, nevertheless, he knew her departure was to be expected. It was getting late and she was with Lily. Since he hadn't planned on pushing any physical contact, he simply watched as she walked ashore and worked her way up the hillside.

"When can I see you again?" Paul bellowed out, still wading in the sparkling water below, once again attempting to wait out his erection. She slid her wet body back into her slip and her white dress and shrugged.

"Ummm. I'll be in town again on Tuesday. At Baker's." Her voice sounded excited as she peered over the edge. She was thrilled that he wanted to see her again.

"That'll be good, Tsu, but when can I see you, where I can actually touch you again as well?" he sarcastically asked. It reminded her of the unusual predicament they were in, seeing how he was white and she was colored. They most certainly couldn't be seen in town together embracing. What was tolerated in Green Hill as opposed to the center of Lexington, was two entirely different things all together.

"Ummm, I'm not sure, but I'll be at the general store on Tuesday, just before five. I can let you know then." She rushed to pick up her things, putting them away in her woven basket. Paul didn't like her response, but he had to accept it. He watched as she woke Lily up and escorted the sleepy girl through the woods, heading towards the Gaines' house.

When Paul could no longer see them, he swam to the bank. His white boxer were more revealing soaking wet. Which was another reason why he waited for the two of them to leave, before he got out of the creek. He quickly climbed up the hillside and put back on his collared shirt and shorts. He re-crossed the rope bridge and made his way back to his truck. Had he found her? He contemplated. Climbing into the driver's seat he sighed.

"Two fucking days 'til I can....look at her. Great!" He sounded frustrated as he started his truck and headed home for the night. He needed to get a few hours of sleep if he could manage it. Mr. Hobbs was expecting him first thing in the morning to break down the stages at the fields.

Chapter 6

Tuesday finally arrived, and it was almost five o'clock, so Paul began putting the finishing touches on his work for the day. He had been rebuilding a picket fence for Mrs. Calhoun, a close friend of Paul's deceased grandmother. Mrs. Calhoun approached Paul with a cool, sweating glass of lemonade in hand.

"All done for the day, Paul?" She could see that he was. He was packing up his tools and tidying up her yard for the day. She handed him the refreshment and fanned herself with her chunky hand.

"Yes ma'am. Looking pretty good, don'tcha think? I'm sure I'll be able to finish tomorrow sometime." He swallowed the entire drink down in one gulp.

"No rush dear. This is fine work." She examined his craftsmanship with her scrutinizing eyes. "Your grandmother would be so proud of you. I miss her so much." Sadness crept onto her hard face. "She had the sweetest soul. Probably from all that honey she use to consume." Paul laughed at her comment. He momentarily reminisced on his grandmother hard at work, or as she would say 'at play' with her bees. "By the way, do you mind if I come ova to get a honey comb or two this weekend?" Mrs. Calhoun inquired.

"You know you're always welcome, Betty. You're practically a second grandmother to me." He leaned in and embraced her with his free arm. "You just be sure to tell folks' bout all my good work, sound fair? I can use all the extra business I can get." Paul enjoyed flirting with the older woman. Mrs. Calhoun also liked having the young man dally with her. She thought it was kind of him to play with an old widow, such as herself.

"You know I will. Idleness is the Devil's playground, so you just keep on staying busy, son." She hugged him and stuffed some money she had wadded up in her bulky hand into his back pocket "Here's your pay. I know you said you wouldn't charge me, but I wouldn't imagine not paying you for such good work. Maybe this will help you towards an engagement ring for a certain red headed young lady we both know." She winked at him, hoping he would slip up with any little tidbit of information about an engagement to Megan. He simply smiled at her.

"Much appreciated, Betty." He handed her back the drinking glass. He kissed her sweetly on the side of her face. "See ya tomorrow, Betty. Same time, same place?" he posed, before heading over to his truck. Paul didn't want to get into a discussion with Mrs. Calhoun about any plans of proposing to Megan. He knew that Mr. Calhoun's praise would get him more business during the summer months while school was not in session. Even if she assumed that all of his hard work was in pursuit of a ring for Megan. What harm would it do to neither confirm nor deny to her what he needed the extra money for? His focus today, however, was on getting to Baker's on time. Despite the fact that the interaction would be brief. He couldn't miss the opportunity to see Tsu again and be close enough to her to breathe in her sweet scent.

~   ~   ~   ~   ~

In her enthusiasm, Tsu and Lily got to the general store a little earlier than they expected. They dropped off another four dozen bars of assorted soap. She was relieved to find that the first batch she had delivered, only days before, was selling and quickly. She knew that in Hartford her soap had been well received, but she was not sure if the Lexington populace could or would appreciate her craft.

"Here is the next delivery, Mr. Baker. How did we do over the weekend?" Tsu politely inquired, but she could already see that she had done well.

"Just set them up in front, like the others. You did very well over the weekend, Ms. Monroe. Folks took a great liken' to your soaps. Were pickin' up two to three bars at a time," he informed her.

"That's great, Mr. Baker. More than half are already gone." Tsu was excited.

"Yup. You and Lily, I expect are gonna be awfully busy this summer," he happily stated.

"I reckon so," Lily replied, looking at the limited bars remaining in the stand.

"We're working daily, Mr. Baker. We'll do our best to keep up with the demand." Tsu hesitated, looking around the store. She couldn't leave yet, Paul hadn't arrived. She needed to stall for more time. "I need a few items before we leave. We're getting low on some of our supplies."

"Sure thing, Ms. Monroe. I have your money in the register. We'll settle up once you get what you need."

"Thanks, Mr. Baker." She and Lily smiled and walked away.

"You're welcome, ladies." Mr. Baker was extremely respectful, even though they were colored. He always treated her with the same respect he would treat any customer, regardless of her race. Lily excused herself and went to sit on the front steps of the store.

Walking away from the counter Tsu found herself wondering how Mr. Baker could be William's father. With all that Lily had told her about William Jr. and from the one abrupt interaction she had had with William. Mr. Baker appeared to be much kinder than his ill-tempered son.

Delaying for more time in the store, Tsu casually walked down the well-organized aisles, pretending to look for items she needed for soap making. When she heard the faded green screen door slam shut, her eyes jolted upwards and found Paul's. He sauntered over nonchalantly in her direction, holding her in his sights.

"Evening, Paul," Mr. Baker politely commented without paying much mind to the young man entering his store.

"Evening, Mr. Baker." He sounded a quick response. He did not want to get into too much dialogue with Mr. Baker either. "Just picking up a few quick items," he also offered not wanting to raise any suspicion.

"Help yourself, son," Mr. Baker replied, while he continued working on the books for the evening.

Tsu was wearing denim shorts, a two-button white shirt and a pair of flats. Her kinky, curly hair was pulled off of her face and wrapped in a bun crowning her head. It was the first time she had worn her natural hair in town. It was becoming too difficult to straighten it every day with the humidity and the all the swimming she and Lily had been doing. Paul still covered with traces of sawdust and heavily scented with sassafras, trailed closely behind Tsu as she made her way through the store. Tsu walked down the plumbing aisle, intending to be out of the eyesight of any persons entering the store and Mr. Baker. She placed a canister of Lye into her basket. Paul followed her down the aisle and positioned his body behind hers. Brushing up against her, he bent over her small frame and whispered into her ear.

"When can I see you, where I can touch you and hold you again?"

Tsu sidestepped away from the welcomed intrusion of her personal space, smiling. She took a glimpse at the cashier's counter at Mr. Baker, hoping not to draw any attention to her and Paul. She reached into her pocket, pulled out a folded piece of white paper and placed it into the palm of Paul's callused hand. She squeezed before she released his hand, as she felt it was the only gesture of affection that could be given to him there. Knowing that Lily was outside the store waiting for her, Tsu turned and proceeded to the counter to pay for her items.

~   ~   ~   ~   ~

Lily was sitting on the steps outside of Baker's, when she spied Willy J. from across the road. His hair and clothes appeared unkept, which was highly unusual for him. He always took great pride in his personal appearance. William didn't say a word to Lily, like he would normally do. He just stared with a grimace on his face, gulping at his flask. Tsu immediately drew his gaze as she walked out of the store, but his facial expression did not change. He looked angered and Tsu thought it best not to put either Lily or herself in his path. It was unclear to her what he might be capable of.

"Come on Lily." She signaled to Lily to turn in the opposite direction down the road for home.

"Hey Lily? How bout I give you that ride we talked about on my way into the store?" Paul hollered. He had planned this ahead of time, knowing that a two minute interaction wouldn't be nearly long enough after waiting two days. So he arranged a ride with Lily, before he walked into Baker's to meet with Tsu. He only knew that he needed more time with her. Also, he had given Lily so many rides home before, that anyone paying attention wouldn't think anything of him giving them a ride now. He hadn't even looked at the folded white note she had given him in the plumbing aisle, just minutes before.

"I already toldja ya could," Lily replied, jumping into the back of the black truck filled with lumber and tools. Paul handed Lily a Coke and a handful of red licorice, before opening the passenger door to let Tsu in. She smiled as he closed her in, becoming fully aware of his intentions to take them home the whole time. He thought himself quite clever, and the smirk on his face said as much to Tsu.

"Paul!" William called out to his friend from across the way. William motioned with his arms, beckoning Paul to come over to him. Paul hadn't even noticed William sitting there when he walked out of Baker's. Although he was eager to be with Tsu, he didn't want to bring any unwanted attention to what was developing between him and Tsu, especially to William. Paul jogged over briskly to his friend, not knowing exactly what to expect. He knew how competitive Willy could be, and how upset he could get when he didn't get his own way.

"Where ya think you're going with my gal?" William stammered out. He came to a full stance and reeked of alcohol. He had obviously been drinking most of the day and Paul knew how even more unruly Willy could be when he was drunk and angry.

"She isn't your girl, Willy. In case you forgot, you're getting married next month to Abby," he cautiously reminded his friend. Paul couldn't stomach William claiming Tsunami for his own. But he also couldn't risk getting into an altercation over it in the middle of town, so he tried reasoning with his friend. "They could use a lift and I'm headed that way."

"Colored gals don't count as cheating, stupid." William remarked, finishing and opening yet another beer. "Besides, I know you heard me say she was mine that day in Randy's car." William got into Paul's face in an aggressive manner.

"You're drunk, Willy," Paul dismissively scoffed. "I'm just giving them a ride home is all." William huffed in disbelief and took a step back.

"What about the other night at the creek? What do ya call what I saw the two of you makin' out in the water doing? Swim lessons?"

"What?" Paul's eyes widened. Hadn't Willy left? Paul thought to himself. He could only actually recall seeing the girls, Randy and Greg leave. Did Willy stay behind?

"You didn't look like you were thinkin' much about Megan either, Mr. High & Mighty. Since we're talkin' morals now," William snickered. Caught off guard by Williams' accusations, Paul simply countered.

"This is neither the time nor the place, and you're drunk, buddy. We'll talk about this another time," he demanded, trying to avoid a scuffle with him in the road. Paul knew William very well. Even before he came to live with his gammy at when he was ten after Paul's parents had died. He was pretty sure that this would not be the end of it, but in the moment Paul just wanted to get back to Tsu. After all, he had been waiting days to see her again, and he had gone through all the trouble of setting up a few more minutes with her. "Sober up, man. I'll come see you later tonight and we can talk about it and clear this whole thing up then." Paul added tapping

William on the shoulder, before turning a foot and making his way back to his truck.

"Sure thing, buddy. What are friends for?" William called out watching Paul running back over to his truck with the two girls. He hopped in the driver's side and ignited the engine.

~ ~ ~ ~ ~

Once in his truck, Paul didn't waste any of his time thinking about William. All he wanted to concentrate on was Tsu's sweet face.

"Is everything alright?" Tsu inquired, referring to the obvious tension between him and William in the street just moments before. Paul pulled out of his parking spot and into the street, heading for the Gaines' residence.

"Yeah, Willy's just drunk and can get a little mouthy when he's had a few too many," he explained, leaving out the important parts of the story. That William had seen the two of them at the creek and wanted Tsu for himself. "I've missed you," he confessed, resting his lengthy hand on her exposed tanned knee. He wanted to change the subject. His eyes closed briefly the second he made contact with her warm, soft skin. It was almost unbearable knowing that that was most likely as far as he was going to be able to go.

"Did you read my note?" she teasingly questioned, trying not to be affected by the tender stroking Paul had started on her leg.

Paul completely forgot about the note she had given him. What he had set up trumped any note he presumed.

"Nope. I couldn't take my eyes off of you once I saw you," he explained. He was using his charm to excuse the fact that he didn't even bother to read the damn thing. Tsu blushed anyway. He liked the effect he was having on her and he continued caressing her exposed thigh. Her skin was smooth and hot. He noticed that she had darkened a little since she arrived in town several weeks back. "You've tanned a bit since you came to Lexington, Tsunami." He noticed! Tsu thought.

"Yes, I have. My mother would say that I have been sun kissed," she offered with a shy smile.

"Sun kissed," he repeated. "I like the way that sounds. But how about being Paul kissed?" he retorted with a sly grin. Tsu blushed even deeper but did not respond to his question. It was difficult to think with his hand stimulating her senses, along with his flirtatious comments.

"Can you meet me tomorrow night?" she managed to mutter out against his arousing touch.

"Of course! Where?" he replied excitedly

"Well, the note that I gave you said that there is a small cabin in the woods, not far from the Hawk's Ledge," she explained. "Lily and I have taken ownership of it, and are using it as our own private little refuge. But you didn't even read it now, did you?" she snapped, while she removed his hand from her thigh. It was assaulting her wit along with her emotions. Shocked and amused,

Paul realized that Tsu had not fallen for his earlier justification for not reading her note. However, charming he had been. He ran his hand through his wild curly brown hair, in order to regain his poise. The gentle stroking had been affecting him as well.

"Tomorrow will be great. I can meet you by 6:30," he informed her.

"That'll be mighty fine, Mr. Morrison," she quipped as they carried on down the road.

"You're mighty fine, Tsunami," he commented grasping and holding her hand for the remainder of the journey.

~　　　~　　　~　　　~　　　~

Once they arrived at the Gaines' home, Lily and Tsu showed Paul the path to the cabin from the house and how he could get there from the cliff. He would have to park his car on the other side of the creek and cross over the rope bridge as he had done before. Once he got to the ledge it would be easy for him to navigate his way to the cabin during the daytime or with a lantern at night. The two ladies escorted Paul back to his truck and they were all holding hands, as they made their way back to the Gaines' home. He agreed to be there tomorrow night to meet Tsu at the cabin. Just then, Mr. Gaines pulled in. Jimmy climbed his large body out of his car, with a look of concern on his stern face.

"Hey Paul. Anthang I can do for ya?" Jimmy Gaines looked troubled to see such a sight. Tsu immediately released Paul's hand, which Paul noticed, but he understood why.

"Not at all, Jimmy uh...Mr. Gaines. I was just dropping off that lumber we discussed you needed for your barn. I saw that your girls needed a lift home, and I was on the way," he explained. Lily smiled wildly, still swinging her and Paul's arms. Uncle Jimmy looked un-amused, looking into the girls faces. Although he suspected that he knew Paul well enough to know that he met the young ladies no harm. "If you give me a hand we can unload it and I can be on my way, sir."

"It's alright, Paul. I completely fogot bout the wood. How bout a beer?" Jimmy offered.

"That would be great, sir." Mr. Gaines went into this house to fetch him and Paul a couple of beers. Paul seized the opportunity to scoop Tsu into his arms, to steal a quick kiss from her. When her father returned to the front porch, Lily was laughing into her cupped hands. Lily was thankful that Paul wasn't trying to hide the feelings he had for Tsu, from her. Uncle Jimmy was completely oblivious to what was going on between them.

"What's so funny, gal?" her father questioned.

"It looks like your fly in undone, sir," Paul countered, flashing Lily a wide-eyed look.

"Yeah, dang zippas busted." The two men unloaded the wood and enjoyed a few beers together. He even helped Jimmy replace a few of the damaged boards in the barn. Every time Mr.

Gaines went into the house for more beer, Paul acquired a kiss from Tsu's willing mouth. Lily thought it was a most amusing game. After finishing a third beer with Jimmy, Paul decided it was time to head home for the evening. A wave had to suffice as a goodbye to Tsu. Mr. Gaines watched as he departed standing alongside Tsu and Lily.

~   ~   ~   ~   ~

William sat on his porch thinking about Paul and Tsu together, another time. Today would be the third time that, they were together that William knew about. He could tell that Paul hadn't taken her yet.

"Pussy," he called out. William thought to himself. He wouldn't have hesitated. Shimmying that white dress up over her waist, he would've fucked her right there on the field house, letting the sounds of the fireworks drown out her cries. The notion intrigued him to the point that he needed to adjust his crotch again. "Paul doesn't even know what to do with a piece like that," William murmured out, downing another beer. "I'll show him how it's done and he can have the remnants once I've expanded her limitations a bit. Paul will thank me in the long run for saving him from her and if he doesn't who gives a shit." Paul was nowhere in sight. He most certainly had forgotten about telling William he would come by and speak with him later that night. William dimmed the lantern he had been sitting by on his porch, but remained rocking in his chair in the darkness.

Chapter Seven

Paul arrived early at the cabin Wednesday night, in order to set up blankets and a picnic basket dinner for the two of them. He was surprised to find two old cots, classic books, shards of soaps and other assorted random items, belonging to Tsu and Lily. He fingered through their belongings, pieces together clues of who Tsu might be. Her whimsical handwritten stories, stitched quilts and scented oils. He found himself wondering if the girls had slept over occasionally in the old cabin as well. It was convenient enough after their late night swims.

~   ~   ~   ~   ~

Tsu arrived at the cabin wearing a shin length green flowing dress with no shoes. She had a bag of cookies she made in hand and her hair was pulled back away from her beaming face. She was astonished by all the trouble Paul had gone through, setting up the little room with dinner for two. He even had candles lit in small reused mason jars. The gesture was rather romantic. She wished she had known that he had planned on making dinner for her. Otherwise, she wouldn't have stuffed herself full with her Aunt Shirley's food beforehand.

Paul walked over to her and lifted her off the ground, twirling her around before placing a tender kiss on her lips. There was something about kissing her, that made him feel more complete. Placing her back down on the cabin's floor, he carefully scanned her figure. He thought that the green dress complemented her sun kissed skin, beautifully.

"Hope you're hungry!" He said, rather excited to have her sample his cooking. The thought of eating another bite revolted Tsu, but he had gone through so much trouble. She did not want to offend or to disappoint him.

"I can eat a little. I brought you some cookies. Made them myself," she informed him, while handing over the bag. He placed them down on the blanket with the rest of the food.

~   ~   ~   ~   ~

They picked at the contents in the basket, all the while talking, laughing and getting to know each other better. What was left of the daylight, soon drifted into dusk.

"Tell me about your family, Tsu," he requested.

"We're not all that interesting," she sighed. "My father passed away from the flu, while on duty in the Navy when I was just a little girl and my mother is a nurse. She works for a grand lady, Mrs. Ellington. They are more like best friends though. She takes my mother on all of her adventures."

"What kind of adventures?" He enjoyed getting her to talk about things that she liked. She would become so vibrantly expressive with her face. It was joyous for him to watch her interact with him.

"Hmmmm, let's see. Right now they are on a tour around Europe." Paul continued to watch Tsu's animated eyes as she talked. They were active, like a child's. She had so much life in her, when the right question was asked. "But they've been to Egypt, Brazil, Canada, Mexico, the Grand Canyon, California and I believe Cuba was their first trip together. Mrs. Ellington likes to travel. Funny thing is, my father promised my mother she'd get to see the world, he was absolutely right. It was in her fate."

"You believe in fate, Ms. Monroe?" Paul was intrigued. Tsu had captivated him.

"I believe in the possibility of all things. I do not think that coincidences are accidents. Some things are fated to happen and the rest is up to us," she confessed. "What do you think, Mr. Morrison?" A sense of relief came over him.

"I believe in fate, destiny, and star-crossed lovers, like us." Tsu embarrassingly smiled at Paul. They hadn't attempted making love yet, and here he was referring to her as his lover. "Let's see what else. Santa Claus, the Easter Bunny and my personal favorite, the Tooth Fairy." He laughed.

"Oh really, and why is that a personal favorite?"

"Anytime a cute chick, wants to sneak into my bedroom at night and also gives me money, would definitely make her my favorite," he confessed.

"And how do you know that she, is in fact a she or that she's cute?"

"My Tooth Fairy is definitely a girl." He shrugged his shoulders. "And any depiction of fairies I've ever seen, they've all been pretty attractive."

"That's very interesting to know."

"What? That fairies are cute?" he wondered. She laughed.

"No. That you like strange female sneaking into your bedroom and that you have crushes on fairies." She leaned in closer to him. "I'm not sure I'm your type," she exclaimed in a soft voice.

"Oh, you are. In more ways than I could've imagine." Paul's statement causes Tsu to blush deeper.

"So, tell me about the Morrison family?" She needed to change the subject, quickly.

"My parents were great. My mom was a school teacher and my dad was actually a carpenter for a living. They died when I was ten, in a car crash. That's when I came back to Lexington to live with my gammy." Tsu listened intently to his story. "Gammy was amazing. I wish she'd gotten a chance to meet you. I know she would've loved you. She died a few years back, from a heart attack. She left me the house and now there's just me. The last Morrison standing."

"So you learned carpentry from your dad?" Tsu inquired.

"Not at all," he replied with remorse. "When I was seventeen I had an accident at Hawk's Ledge. Hence why I know about the rocks on the bottom. Anyway, I might not have made it if it weren't for this boy, Nathaniel Hobbs, who pulled me to safety. As a result, Hobbs died saving me and I spent every spare moment I had with his folks, helping them out however I could. By coincidence or fate,

Nathaniel's father turned out to be a carpenter. Everything I know was and is still taught to me by Mr. Hobbs in Green Hill. He's been a great friend and teacher to me."

"Lily told me a little about a colored boy saving your life," Tsu confessed.

"I'm sure she did. If you want to know something that's going on in town, ask Lily. I'm not sure how she does it, but she seems to know everything that happens here." Paul sounded fascinated talking about Lily's uncanny ability. Tsu rolled up the sleeve of his t-shirt on his right arm.

"So these scars on your shoulder and arm, are from that accident?" She gently caressed his healed over skin, as she leaned in closer to get a better look.

"They are." He liked having her closer to his body. "I'm hideously disfigured for life." They both laughed. He removed his shirt completely, so that she could see the surgical scars wrapping around his shoulder. His half naked body was overwhelmingly appealing to her and she needed to change the subject again.

"Would you like a cookie, Paul? They're butter cookies." She untied the ribbon on the bag and place it before him. He could tell that she had become enthralled with his physique but also uncomfortable with feeling so. He pulled his t-shirt back over his frame.

"Sure!" He pulled out one of the golden, sand dollar cookies and bit into it. Immediately, he began spitting pieces of the chewed up cookie out. "This might be the worst thing I ever tasted," he snickered. Tsu was embarrassed.

"What's wrong with them? I worked really hard on trying to make them perfect." She was frazzled. Paul took a swig of his cola.

"I'd say you used too much baking soda. They smell great, look great, but they are truly, truly awful, Tsu," he teased. "The absolute worst thing I think I've ever eaten." Tsu began to laugh at herself. She knew she was a terrible cook. "I'm pretty good at cooking, maybe you should let me do it from here on out.

"Deal. That sounds like the best thing for the both of us," she reinforced. They were beginning to become comfortable with one another.

Her smell and her proximity to him was affecting him, but he had no idea what if any previous experiences she had had. His curiosity was getting the better of him and he wanted to know about her sexual history. If she even had one that was. He knew that she had been engaged before, but wondered how far she had gone with a man.

"Have you ever been with a man before, Tsu? Like in a physical way?" The question caught her off guard. She wasn't embarrassed by it, but she was concerned about what his expectations for her might be.

"Wallace and I were intimate on occasion, before he left that is," she disclosed making a funny grimace. She wasn't ready to tell him how inadequate she had been to her ex-fiancé.

"How about you, Paul?"

"I've been with three women. Megan whom you know about, Samantha my college girlfriend and Cecelia, my first." He looked off in the distance fondly remembering Cecelia. "She taught me a great deal about women," he admonished.

"She seems like she was very important to you and in the practice of giving out lessons as well. How very fortunate for you." Paul didn't want for Tsu to be intimidated by someone from his past. His objective and priority was that he wanted her to feel comfortable with him.

"She's in the past. Don't worry," he assured her. "I don't want you to feel pressured into doing anything you don't want to do. When you're ready, we'll take the next step. And if it takes a while, I'm willing to wait for you, Tsu. As long as it takes." She relocated herself back to her spot, adjacent from him. She anxiously crossed her arms across her chest. Naturally, she began closing herself off from him.

"That's comforting to know, Paul." He could sense that the conversation was making her uneasy, so he chose to change the subject once again.

"Tell me bout making soap."

"It's not that interesting, I assure you. Just something I..." Paul interrupted her.

"How could anything you do, not be interesting? You should stop selling yourself short all the time. It doesn't become you," he enforced. "How'd you get into it?" he asked her once again.

"You are very charming, Mr. Morrison. I'll give you that." She released her arms back to her sides. "Mrs. Ellington taught me when I was younger and I've recently picked it up again," she admitted. She put on her storytelling voice, as she began to describe the process to him. "First, we mix lard and oils and then add in scents. Oh yeah and lye. Which you have to be extremely careful with because it will burn you if it gets on your skin, see." She pointed to a small discolored scar on her arm. "Hideously disfigured as well." They both smiled. "Then we cook it and once it gets to a certain temperature, we pour it into molds. At this stage it has to sit for a few weeks before it is ready to be sold or use."

"It just can't be enjoyed once it's cooled down, huh?" he playfully asked.

"Oh no. It needs time to cure. The process cannot be rushed or you would just have subpar, mushy soap," she teasingly responded.

"Wow! Fascinating!" He responded sarcastically. "I did not realize what it actually took to make a bar of soap."

"Don't tease me." She pushed him on his shoulder. "I told you it wasn't very interesting."

"You were right. It does sound pretty boring, but I'd like to help you with a batch one of these days, if that's okay with you?"

"Sure! If you would like," she responded. Paul leaned in closer.

"I very much would," he confessed before sacrificing the conversation to kiss her sweet lips.

~ ~ ~ ~ ~

Every couple of days they would meet at the Cabin and Lily would join them most of the time, as long as it wasn't too late in the evening. Tsu liked having her there as a buffer and Paul didn't seem to mind. She made sure from that first meeting on not to fill up on her Aunt Shirley's cooking, so that she could enjoy Paul's food. He was a pretty good cook for a man. Much better than Tsu by far. Besides cooking up batches of soaps, she could barely boil a pot of water. Many tea kettles were ruined due to her forgetfulness and over boiling the water out of them. Paul was a natural with cooking and flavors. Just as she was with scenting and soap making. All of their secret rendezvous' afforded them the opportunity of getting to know one another better, while they were falling in love with each other.

~ ~ ~ ~ ~

As Tsu was readying herself to leave Paul on one particular occasion, she knew that their relationship was getting dangerously closer to becoming physical. He had been familiarizing himself with as much of her body as she had granted him access too. Paul wouldn't be able, even if he was willing, to hold out much longer and neither would she. Their close, isolated gatherings were unmistakably leading them into a more intimate relationship. On the way home walking through the woods, she dreaded thinking about not being able to satisfy Paul, and how disconnected she was from her own sexuality. She contemplated ending things, but that thought upset her even more than the prospect of disappointing him.

~　　　~　　　~　　　~　　　~

Once she snuck back into the house and found her way to her bed, Lily who was still awake, sat up on her bed. She wanted to discuss some important matters that had been on her mind with Tsu.

"Were you with Paul again?" she asked, fully aware of the answer.

"It's late. You shouldn't be up still, Lily," she responded, startled by Lily's presence.

"It's too hot to sleep. How's Paul tonight? Does he smoke cigarettes, Tsu?" she inquired. Lily knows entirely too much about everything. Not just about me and Paul but everyone's business in Lexington, Tsu considered.

"It is hot, and Paul's fine. And I don't think that he does. At least I've never seen him or smelled tobacco on him. Why do you ask?" Tsu questioned, slipping out of her clothes and into a short light weight nightgown for bed.

"Nothin' important. I just came cross some cigarette butts near the cabin's all," Lily offered.

"Must've been hunters. Or maybe ghosts, from the true owners of the cabin in the woods," Tsu answered. She creepily wiggled her fingers around walking towards the little girl in bed.

However, Lily was not amused, and her face told Tsu as much. She had more pressing things on her mind to talk about.

"How's it feel to be kissed Tsu? Like how Paul kisses you?" Tsu took a deep breath in and exhaled.

"Well I've only ever been kissed by two other men, and it was very different than being kissed by Paul. When he kisses me I feel like I'm floating and falling at the same time. It's both wonderful and frightening," Tsu described. "I feel awakened from a slumber I didn't even know I was in."

"What's sex like?" Lily inquired. Stupefied by Lily's question, Tsu didn't have any idea how to answer it or yet, if she even should. Lily was rather young and how did Tsu know what it was actually like? It's like watching yourself being a part of something you're not even connected too. Like having an out of body experience. These were the first things that came to her mind, and her mood shifted again.

"Lily, I'm not sure you're old enough for this conversation, but what I can tell you, is that it's supposed to be something special you share with someone you love and who loves you. Otherwise, it can be like nothing at all, you can feel like nothing." Her faced pained with regret and Lily could tell Tsu was recollecting a memory from her past.

~   ~   ~   ~   ~

"Once when I was just a few years older than you are now, sixteen. A colored man working at a factory in Hartford grabbed me on my way home from school one day. One of his enormous, filthy hands covered almost my entire face, and the scent of machinery oil intoxicated my nostrils. His other hand held a small dull blade to my throat. He dragged me into an abandoned section of the factory. Forcing me down on the icy cold concrete floors, he spread my legs apart with his heavy body. 'Shhhh. Don't say nuthin or I'll cutcha', he said, while tearing off my underwear. I was so afraid." Tsu's eyes watered with tears, as she hesitated. "I could feel the pressure from him trying to jam himself inside of me. Finally he broke me, and began forcefully thrusting into me hard, for what felt like an eternity". Tears streamed down her grave face, as she explained the offense further.

"The pain is barely describable. Sharp, jabbing blows, one after another to the lower abdomen. I thought he was actually stabbing me with his blade, until I went numb. Then in crept this feeling of nothingness. I was nothing of consideration to him. I wasn't me. It was like I was watching myself and I was just a hole. A means to an end for him, because I was there." Tears continued to flow and she gasped for another breath. "A very precious thing stolen. Not only my virginity and my right to consent. He stole me away. I could feel my hopes and dreams draining out of me, along with the tears escaping the assault." She swiped at her face, smearing the fallen teardrops across her dismal face. "The weight of his smelly body kept me in place long enough for him to finish his

106

business. Once he was able to catch his breath again, he warned me to keep my mouth shut. He threatened that the same thing would happen to my mother, and that the next time he said he might not spare his blade. I knew at that moment that he knew me and had planned his attack." She swiped at her face once again before speaking again.

"It felt as if he had raped away my soul, as I laid on the concrete paralyzed in pain and fear. After a while, I somehow I mustered up the strength or the willpower to get up. But it was long after he had gone. I remember it was dark by then. I bled and ached all the way home. My mother bathed me that night and tried to console me as much as a mother could in that situation, I suppose. 'The curse of a woman,' she said. 'Some men don't ask.' She held me in her arms with my tears spilling into the steamy tub. Since then, I've been just a glimmer, momma would say, of the girl that I used to be. I'm extremely uncomfortable with the idea of having sex now, Lily. Even Wallace experienced my awkwardness, which was most likely one of the reasons for him leaving me. The idea of having to be bound to a sexually lifeless woman the rest of his days, certainly sent him seeking his freedom from me. Wallace knew I was damaged goods and Paul will know too if we keep going the way that we are." She turned away from Lily and laid down on her bed. "He will find me inadequate as well." This was the last thought Tsu had before closing her eyes and crying herself to sleep. Lily was saddened by Tsu's story and what she had gone through. She thought it best not to trouble her with any other questions or concerns. Lily knew that Tsu was in love with Paul. The wisdom beyond her years told her that Tsu was grieving the possibility of losing him.

Chapter Eight

William and Megan, along with their other friends sat at their usual spot on the bank of the creek one hot late July evening. The bonfire was ablaze and everyone's hand was filled with a beer. Paul and Abby were the only usual suspects missing from the group. None of them, except for William, knew where Paul now spent most of his days. And Abby was in Alexandria making the final altercations on her gown for her and William's upcoming wedding. William, who had been drunk incessantly most of the time, knew what Paul had been up to. In his inebriated state, he decided to let Megan in on Paul's whereabouts as of lately. He inched closer to the disheartened lady.

"Our good friend Paul has gotten himself all smitten with that colored gal soloist from the Fourth of July, Megan. That's why none of us has seen him much outside of the Friday games. He's been spending any free time he's got in Green Hill with her," William confessed. Megan was in disbelief.

"He's doing what? With what girl?" Megan exclaimed.

"I just thought you should know, sweetheart, that Paul's been fancying the darker persuasion lately," William added, hoping to discombobulate Megan's already frail mindset.

"I don't understand this. I'm the best catch in the county! He must just be getting it out of his system, right? I know how some of you white men fancy a tumble in the hay with those gals now and again. He'll be back. Hell, even I know bout your assorted affairs with the coloreds, even if Abby won't admit to them." Megan downed another beer. William didn't appreciate her accusation or her tone with him.

"Not so sure it's as simple as that, Megan. You know Paul's not like that," he tried reminding her about Paul's character." He hasn't fucked her yet. He just hangs out with her and that lil' shit, Lily Gaines," William disclosed.

"That must be what it is. The lil' tease is holdin' out. Paul's just there until he gets what he wants from her. I'm sure once he does he'll come back, right?" Megan was looking to William for answers, but she was out of her mind with grief.

Outraged at the thought that a nigger and the soloist was the one occupying all of Paul's time, Megan became almost as intoxicated as William. In doing so, she allowed herself to become more and more vulnerable to him. He thought it might be a perfect opportunity to have a little fun.

"We're gonna head out now. You ready to go, Megan?" Joy asked Megan.

"It's alright, Joy. I'll take Megan over to Abby's. She's pretty drunk, but we got some wedding details to go over still," William remarked.

"Suits us," Greg and Randy commented.

"We hate carrying the drunk bitch anyways," Randy added. The two couples made their way to their cars. Once they were alone, William regarded his emotionally injured prey. Drunk, distraught and disheveled.

"How could he be so careless with someone as remarkable as you?" he commented, gliding his hand upward under her skirt. Megan's senses responded instantly to William's touch. It had been weeks since Paul had touched her. Her body was starving for the attention. "Now, I'm not going to love you as he does," he revealed. He gripped her neck, lowering her down on the bank while reddening her shoulder with his bite. Devastation and desperation were her undoing. Hiking up her skirt to her waist and just barely lowering his own trousers, he sank into Megan's eager sex. William plowed into Megan furiously on the sandy banks of the creek. He declared to her that they would get Paul back for what he was doing.

Neither one of the two had any real attraction to each other, but the circumstances permitted them with a way of dealing with his anger and her grief deep in each other's loins. Megan was inconsolable. The idea that she could be replaced by a colored girl, and to throw salt on an open wound, the soloist was unbearable for her. She knew that white men often like to roll around in the dark with colored women. It was an unspoken reality, especially in the South. But hell, even William wasn't about to turn on his own kind, as it appeared Paul was doing. Surely he would come to his senses soon.

~   ~   ~   ~   ~

It was a ferociously hot July day and Paul had just completed repairing an old oak staircase at the schoolhouse. To his surprise, he

111

was done much earlier than he had anticipated. His thoughts immediately went to his Tsunami, and how she had promised to show him how to make soap. It was just about noon and he was sure that she would be preparing batters, seeing how her demand had increased to several local stores in the county. Paul knew that Jimmy would be at the butcher shop all day and that her Aunt Shirley would be at the beauty salon until after six. Paul could easily hop in his truck and go visit Tsu and Lily for a little while without anyone being aware of it. It was decided. He would go and get his lesson.

~   ~   ~   ~   ~

Paul pulled into the driveway of the small white house, and stepped out of his truck into the sweltering heat. He heard bustling and music coming from the old gray, peeling barn just beyond the house. Walking through the barn door, Paul couldn't help to notice Tsu, before she became aware of his presence there. She was pouring hot mixtures of soap batter into small wooden compartment. A small metal fan circulated hot air throughout the barn. Tsunami was wearing her denim high-waisted shorts and a white buttoned down shirt knotted tightly behind her back. Paul was taken aback when he observed that Tsu wasn't wearing a bra. And because of the scorching heat, she was perspiring so profusely that her brown nipples soaked through her dampened white blouse. His member grew quickly at the sight of her sweaty, hot, scarcely clothed frame. Her hair was held loosely in a bun, in a crown on her

112

head. The old barn smelled incredibly fragrant, like Tsu smelled most of the time. He had become very familiar with her smell. It was a combination of all the scents she used in her soap making.

"Hello, Soap Goddess," Paul revealed himself, startling her in the process of scraping out one of the pans she was working with.

"Paul!" She called out. "You scared me half out of my mind." Tsu suddenly became very aware of how she looked, when Paul's eyes fixed on her very visible breast. She crossed her arm over her chest and took hold of her triceps as she nervously twiddled her right fingers.

"I wanted to have some kind of effect on you, Tsunami, but scaring you is the last thing I had in mind," he informed her leaning over to kiss her on her collarbone. She was salty and sweet and he was aroused by the heat exuding off of her sticky skin. "Where is Lily?" Paul did a quick sweep around the barn with his eyes, trying to locate their young chaperone.

"She got tired from all the work and the heat, so she went into the house for a nap," Tsu explained. He planted more kisses across her neckline and glided his hands along the sides of her arms.

"Did she now?" His eyes widened as he raised an eyebrow. His imagination began spinning. He pulled her to his lips, as he had done so many times before. He raised his hand and cupped her left breast and she inhaled sharply, as if she was afraid. Paul could see her apprehension.

"May I?" With reluctance, she nodded yes. Tsu knew where this would lead them, and to her surprise she was afraid yet eager to explore it further.

He filled his large hands with each of her breasts and some of her flesh still managed to spill out the sides of his grasp. Paul's eyes stayed focus on Tsu's conflicted face, while his hands explored her body. Her eyes only left his for the occasional eye roll, when he stroked a sensitive spot. Her reaction to his touch was even more so arousing than how she looked.

"Tsunami, I want you more than anything right now but if you say no, I won't press on or force you to continue." His desire was evident from his labored breathing. Placing his mouth against her forehead he asked "May I have you? Here? Now?" Moving his forehead against hers, it was a plea. Tsu was overwhelmed and consumed with love for him. He needs me, she thought. And because I love him, I need to give myself to him. Even if it means the end of us.

"Yes, Paul. I am yours." She threw her arms around him and let some of her inhibitions go. The words were Paul's undoing. He unbuttoned every button of her damp shirt and let it fall to her sides, revealing her naked breast. He took a moment to regard her body. His faced pained with the thought that she was the most beautiful thing he'd had ever seen. Next, he undid the button and unzipped her shorts. He slowly slid them down, kneeling in the process in order to remove them from around her ankles. He paused before he had the chance to do so completely. To his astonishment, Tsu had not been wearing any under garments at all. There he was, unexpectedly facing her bare sex. It was almost unbearable for him to continue on with his slow quest. He looked to Tsu's embarrassed face, as if he were seeking an explanation from her.

"It was much too hot for any underwear today," she spoke softly. When he managed to find the vigor to stand back up to his feet, he did not ravage her like she had assumed he would. Paul just looked at her. She was mostly naked, scared and beautiful, but he needed her to be comfortable with him. For her to want it, and to want him.

"Tsunami, I need to know that you want me too." He started taking off his clothes one article at a time until he stood before her naked. He was glorious to her, and his erection was ready to penetrate deep inside her.

Adonis, she thought.

"I won't touch you unless you asked me too, Tsu. But you can touch me if you want," he informed her. Tsu stepped closer to him walking into the tip of his erection with her flesh. A shock wave shot through his body at the first contact his member made with her body. She rubbed her fingers through the sparse brown hairs on his chest. He watched her intensely and she began kissing his chest and then his neck leading up to his bristly jaw line. Tsu had never touched a man like she was doing now. Finding his lips, she pushed her tongue into his mouth trying to exhibit her need for him. Suddenly, she pulled herself back. She was uncertain of what she was supposed to do next.

"Paul, I want to make you feel wanted, but I don't know what I'm supposed to do. I need you to show me," Tsu confessed, even more embarrassed by her admitted lack of know how. Paul realized that her apprehension was not from being uncertain if she wanted to be with him, but that she didn't have the experience to know what to do with a man. Still, he knew she had been involved with one before.

"I'll show you, he told her." Paul scooped her up folding her legs around his waist, and quickly carried her over to some bales of hay stacked neatly in the corner of the barn. He lowered her body on the cubed bundles. Sensing his urgency excited her, and she could feel the heat building in her womb as her sex moistened. Paul kissed her torso passionately as she wiggled and writhed beneath his assault. The sight of her enjoying his touch aroused him so much, and he knew that he would not be able to hold out much longer. He wanted her to need for him to be inside of her, as he needed to be inside of her. He stood above her, his erection just inches from her sex.

"Tsunami, are you ready?" Sliding a finger in and out of her wet, warm opening and then adding another finger. "My God, you're pretty small, Tsu!" His need grew even greater.

Between breaths she replied "Yes! I think I'm ready." She didn't know if she was or not. She only knew that it never felt like this before with anyone. She had never felt like this before.

"I'll go slowly at first. Let me know if I'm hurting you in anyway and I'll stop okay?" he reassured her.

116

"Okay," she assured him. He parted her legs further apart, giving him more access to her. He withdrew his fingers from her bloom. He positioned his tip against her opening and slowly pushed inward, until he sank into her filling her deeply. Tsu moaned out of pain initially. The stretching and the fullness was a lot to bare as she could feel him in her belly, hurting and oddly feeling pleasurable as well.

Paul moved back and forth, in and out slowly allowing Tsu to find some comfort with him. He soon picked up the pace when he felt her tense body relax, as she adjusted to his girth and his thrusts. He was thankful she was being so responsive to him, because he didn't think he would be able to continue for too much longer. The way she felt. Watching and listening to her sounds, in what he hoped was satisfaction. After a while it had all become too much for him to handle and he spilled his seed deep into her womb. Tsu could feel his pulsating member as he emptied into her and she liked the way its spasm felt against her inner parts. Paul collapsed to her chest. Exhausted and relieved, he apologized to Tsu.

"I didn't mean to finish before you had a chance too. It was really difficult to keep going with what I was dealing with," he disclosed. "You feel incredible, Tsu. I didn't know you would feel like that," he confessed, while he was still inside of her. Tsu however was very much aroused, but she wouldn't allow herself to believe what he was saying about how she felt to him. And even though she had not climaxed, she experienced much more than she had ever done so before. She felt every aspect of him, and enjoyed the feeling of him moving inside of her. Rubbing her hands up and down his spine she became aware of his growing erection still planted between her legs.

"May I have you again?" he begged with yearning in his eyes. Before she could answer, he shifted their bodies backwards into one of the old chairs in the barn. Seated on his lap he said, "I want you to try it like this. I think you'll be able to get more out of this position." Trusting him completely Tsu, barely able to touch the ground with her toes, she began rising and falling on the shaft of his erection. Both of them could not contain their sighs, relishing in her grip to his glide. Paul guided her hips by moving her up and down on his lap. He started to feel her muscles squeezing and shuddering on his shaft. She was reacting to everything, and feeling something inside of her building. She let out a moan. Paul knew her body was close to orgasm, so he continued guiding her up and down, quickening her rise and her fall. She naturally began to roll her hips with little direction from him. She was enjoying him. All of him and he was enjoying watching her uncover her own sexuality with and possibly because of, him. It was obvious to Paul now, that no one had brought it out of her before. Her body began to tremor uncontrollably as she exploded all around him, finding her release. Paul having never witnessed such an aggressive climax before, could no longer control his own impeding orgasm and he drained all that he had into Tsu once more.

Arching her body backwards, Paul caught Tsu before she fell off of his lap. She was delirious with pleasure and opening her eyes they seemed to radiate from a satisfaction she had never known.

Tsu peered into Paul's face, heavy and full with amazement. She held his face into her hands and placed her forehead to his.

"How have you done these things to me?" she questioned, realizing that he had just awakened something deep and dormant inside of her. Would she ever be able to walk away from him now?

Paul had no response for her. He felt that in all actuality, she was the one that had affected and had changed him. After allowing her to catch her breath, he picked her body up and off of his and placed her down onto the chair. His lack of a response, troubled her. Had she said something wrong? He slipped back into his shorts and retrieved a cold bottle of coke from the old icebox in the barn.

"Did I hurt you?" he inquired, while resting the cold bottle between her legs. She jolted from the chilliest of the glass bottle upon her engorged lips at first. But she appreciated the relief it brought to her swollen, hot, lower parts.

"I'm a little sore now, but I've never experienced anything like that before," she replied. Overpowered by her emotions, strains of salty tears ran down her face. She was struggling with a conflict between how she felt and what she was thinking. Why hadn't he responded to her question?

"I've never felt anything like that either, Tsu. That was the most amazing experience I have ever had," he confessed. He wiped away her fallen tears, while still holding the bottle in place. "You seem to astonish me in every way, Tsu."

Tsu blushed. She was mostly embarrassed by the lack of control she had over her bodily functions, but she wanted to believe he was being sincere. He leaned in close to kiss her full lips.

"Let's get you dressed, beautiful." Paul helped her put back on the clothes he had previously removed from her body, before their interlude. While he was buttoning the last button on her shirt, a few stray pieces of hay fell from the loft of the barn. Their faces tensed.

"Lily!" Tsu shouted. "Have you been up there the whole time?" Tsu was appalled and outraged.

"I was sleep in the loft and woke up when I heard funny noises. By that time, you two were...well already makin' love," Lily nervously responded. Tsu was mortified. She looked to Paul as she was even more embarrassed by Lily's presence, and found that he was laughing. With a questioning face, Tsu demanded a response from him, but Paul just shrugged.

"Not much we can do now, Tsu. Lily is always around. She's become the witness to our lives." He pulled Tsu into him. "To our love."

Tsu felt her world spin. Did he just say love?

Chapter Nine

After that day in the barn, Paul, Tsunami and Lily were practically inseparable. The three of them would meet at Hawk's Ledge to swim or in the barn to make soap. They all especially liked having picnics at the cabin and would do so whenever they finished their work for the day. Lily had indeed become their witness. She watched the two them daily, falling deeper in love with each other. She had never seen anything like the two of them. It was as if time slowed down for them and the world didn't exist outside the three of them. However, Paul and Tsu did make certain to have time just for themselves once in a while. Lily only minded a little. She understood that the two of them needed their privacy to do more grown up things.

~   ~   ~   ~   ~

One late night alone at the cabin, Tsu had become rather curious about the little cabin they had taken over, and what it had been used for in the past. While they laid on one of the old cots, Tsu held her resting head to Paul's chest. She listened to the sound of his beating heart, wondering if he had any prior knowledge about the cabin.

"Paul?" she asked, running her hand delicately through the sparse hairs on his chest. His hands glided up and down the length of her spine. Just a sheet draped across their bodies through the moonlit window. "What do you think this cabin was used for?" Paul wasn't exactly sure, but he made an educated guess. The probable answer made him feel uncomfortable. It reminded him that things weren't as easy and perfect as they were pretending them to be, all of these weeks.

"This land use to be all plantations, Tsu. Originally, I reckon it was one of many slave quarters." He felt ashamed and uncomfortable just from saying it. She became aware that his explanation for the cabin's purpose, had changed his mood. She decided to make light of the situation. She pushed herself up from his chest and looked adoringly into his shame filled face.

"So does that make me your slave?" she teased, slowly walking her index and middle fingers up his defined chest. He laughed in amusement at the thought of it.

"No, Tsunami." Tsu began to love the way Paul used her full name, especially when they were making love. "I am, and have always been your slave," he sincerely proclaimed. Tsu was dumbstruck and completely pleased by this man. Her bashful smile told him as much, even though she spoke no words. She simply laid her head back down over his heart to listen and to feel it beat further. Paul enjoyed having her resting upon him and he held onto her, like he treasured her. She had revived him in ways he was starting to believe weren't possible. After a few minutes of quietness, Paul opened his mouth to break the silence.

"Tsu, there has been something I've been meaning to ask you," he sounded, nervously.

"Ask away, Adonis." She adoringly referred to her lover, continuing to twirl her fingers through the scant brown hairs of his chest. Upon hearing her response a smile appeared on his rugged face and he looked relieved.

"Will you come spend the night with me, at my home this Saturday?" he requested. Tsu sat up, pulling the sheet to her chest, in efforts to keep her body covered.

"But how are we to do that?" she inquired. She knew that it would be a scandal if the town folk knew that they were together in the capacity they had become accustomed too. It was one thing for a white man to creep over into Green Hill, but completely different to bring the coloreds home.

"I know that it's kinda dangerous, but your aunt and uncle will be going away to Raleigh this weekend, and William will be getting married this Saturday. Almost the entire town will be at that wedding until late. No one will be around." He pushed himself up looking into her distressed face, before continuing. "I can leave early during the reception and meet you at the post office. I promise to get you back early Sunday before anyone knows that you were there." He had it all figured out. It had been on his mind for the past week and he really wanted to be with Tsu, in his home and in his bed. The idea of it was troubling to her, but she could not resist his pleading playful eyes or deny his request.

"Of course I'll stay with you in your home," she responded. "What kind of master would I be, if I did not look after the request of my one and only slave?" she quipped. Paul rolled her up in his arms appreciating her good humor. He was so pleased that she had agreed to spend the night with him, that they made love once again on the small cot in the cabin.

~   ~   ~   ~   ~

Saturday early evening, the day of William and Abby's wedding, people were bustling about the church half an hour before the ceremony. Paul, in spite of everything remained as William's best man. Though he had neglected almost all of his best man's duties over the past several weeks. To no one's surprise, Megan was Abby's maid of honor. They had been friends since their sophomore year of college. Abigail was the very reason Megan and Paul had met and gotten together.

Before the ceremony began, Megan managed to corner Paul into one of the small church holding quarters. She needed to confront him about his whereabouts over the past several weeks leading up to the wedding. Paul had abandoned pretty much all of his normal activities except for the baseball games. Even then he was distant and isolated himself from the group. Megan had fully expected a proposal by now, on the wake of her best friend's wedding. She had assumed that this affair would have run its course by now. Paul's truck had been seen increasingly more often heading towards Green Hill. People were starting to gossip about why he was spending so much of his time there. Not to mention the obvious fact, that he had been completely neglecting her, so the prospects of marriage were beginning to seem bleak. He looked very handsome to her in his navy suit. Although his facial hair was much longer than she'd prefer. However, she wasn't here to be distracted by his grooming or lack thereof, she wanted answers and restoration.

"What's going on, Paul? What are you doing to us?" she demanded, not really knowing how he would answer her questions. She attempted to be poised in her soft pink dress, modest make-up and up do. "There's been lots of talk bout your truck being in Green Hill a lot or at the creek all of the time now. Not to mention, that you don't hang out with any of your friends anymore." Paul just listened. He did not want to hurt Megan and he didn't know what he could say, that wouldn't do just that. "Your actions are causing me a great deal of embarrassment, Paul. I fully expected a proposal by now, but when I am in town, you're nowhere to be found. What are you doing, Paul?" Her sorrowful eyes pleaded with his for an answer. She wanted for him to beg her for her forgiveness and to vow to be only hers for all of eternity.

Paul looked into her watery eyes. He knew that he wouldn't be able to give Megan what she wanted, even though she still conveyed the prospect of hope. The last thing he dreamed of doing, was to hurt her. But he could no longer bare to keep the reality of the situation from her. He was never going to marry Megan O'Shea. It had been blaringly evident to him for some time that there was a deficit in their relationship. And when he found Tsu, what had been missing with Megan, was realized and within his grasp to obtain. He wasn't about to let that go now that he found it.

125

"I'm sorry, Megan, you're right. You deserve an explanation. You deserved one weeks ago. The truth is, I've fallen in love with someone else." Just like ripping off a Band-Aid he thought. He considered that quickest would be best. The words hit her like a punch in the gut. Megan had no idea that he could be capable of loving that colored gal. Especially since he had had her all of this time.

"In love!" She howled. "In love. With that nigger bitch from the solos?" She slapped him hard across his bearded face, with her perfectly manicured hand. His words were an insult to her. Paul didn't react to the physical assault. He knew how much his confession had to be hurting Megan in the moment. She keeled over and cradled her stomach. "How can this be? You've only just met her! Haven't you been in love with me?" she insisted, gripping at the ache assaulting her belly. Paul wanted to reach out and console her, but he didn't want to risk her confusing his intentions in the situation. "We all know you've been fucking the lil' whore, but God, in love…." Her harsh words trailed off as tears raced down her face.

"Don't speak about her like that or call her anymore names, Megan," Paul firmly stated. He was serious. "Last thing I ever wanted to do was to cause you any harm, but there has always been something not quite right about us, way before Tsunami. We were broken long before her, so I'm not gonna let you stand here, blame or talk about her like that."

"Tsunami? You're not gonna let me talk about that trash? How could you do this to me?" Megan raised her hand to slap him again, even harder than the first blow, as the sting of his request pained her. But he caught her wrist before she could make contact with his face again and he jolted her body backwards a few steps.

"It's over, Megan. I suggest that you try and pull yourself together. Our friends are getting married today." He exited the small quaint room offering no other sympathy or comfort. He could tolerate no more insults to his beloved Tsunami. He knew there was nothing he could do to mend Megan's broken heart or her bruised ego. Also, he knew that Megan would never be able to understand or except him choosing another woman over her. Specifically, a colored one. Paul on the other hand, was no longer concerned with the color of Tsu's skin. He just saw Tsu, simple and for everything that she was.

~   ~   ~   ~   ~

Shattered by Paul's confession, Megan quickly found her way to William. He was occupying another private chamber in the church with his buddies. He dismissed Randy and Greg when he saw how frazzled she looked. Once they were alone, she told him all that Paul had disclosed to her.

"I am well aware of how things have progressed between the two of them, Megan. I tried to tell you that things might be more serious. Paul's not really a fling kinda guy. Christ, I heard he practically dated that whore he lost his virginity to," William confessed. He regarded her through his mirror while he readied himself. She was falling apart, as he tied his navy bow tie to perfection.

"I don't understand why this is happening, William. I don't think I can get through the day." Her confession annoyed him. He couldn't have her current emotional state interfering with or ruining his big day. He had big plans for the evening. He approached her.

"Listen here. You have got to pull yourself together for Abby's sake." He reached into his jacket pocket and pulled out a handful of white pills. He did not appreciate how selfish she was acting. "Here, take two of these." He offered Megan some valium to calm herself down, and as William waited for it to kick in, he lapsed into a memory from several weeks prior to his wedding.

~   ~   ~   ~   ~

After waiting for Paul on his porch the night he never showed, William decided he needed to keep a closer eye on him. In doing so, he discovered the two lovers' secret meeting spot just beyond the cliff. He would watch and study their interactions with one another. He convinced himself that he was mostly there, waiting for his opportunity to bring Tsu to her knees. However, the very last time William had gone to the cabin, was the first time he saw Tsu and Paul making love. Even though it angered him, he was envious over the connection they seemed to have made. Why couldn't someone touch me like that? Want me like that?

"Why Paul?" he deliberated with himself. Taking his last few pulls of his cigarette, he watched as they both came undone in the cabin. He dropped the cigarette butt to the ground pivoting his toe aggressively, to put the damn thing out. "Where gonna have our day Tsu, real soon." Walking away from the cabin, William disappeared into the night's protective cloak.

~   ~   ~   ~   ~

Pulling himself back from his memory, William lifted Megan's' head.

"He's gonna pay. They're both gonna pay," he promised Megan. "After I get back from my honeymoon in Savannah and New Orleans in two weeks. I'll take care of everything, darling."

In her loopy, relaxed state, Megan kissed William on the lips and thanked him for being such a good friend to her. William pushed her down and away from his mouth and stood before her. He unzipped his pants. "Now cheer up darling. I'm getting married today," he announced, while pushing her head into his crotch.

~   ~   ~   ~   ~

The ceremony was quick and lovely. At the reception everyone was having a grand time, even Megan. With the combination of drugs and alcohol she had coursing through her system she appeared to be having the most fun of all. Paul stayed just long enough to give his best man speech, giving credit to Abby for taking on the role as the new Mrs. William J. Baker.

"I've known Willy for a long time now, and he is the luckiest fellow I have ever met, but also the cleverest. How he managed to convince an angel like Abigail Ridley to say I do, surely heaven only knows. But I do know that he is at his best with her. So, I would like to pay homage to Abigail, for willingly taking on the role of the new Mrs. William J. Baker. May your burdens be delightful. Cheers!" Paul raised his glass and all the other guests raised their glasses to the newlyweds as well. Once the dancing commenced, Paul saw his opportunity to depart undetected. Discarding his navy suit jacket and bow tie, he hopped into his truck and headed to the post office, where his Tsunami would surely be waiting.

~ ~ ~ ~ ~

At the Gaines' house, Aunt Shirley scrambled to the car with her overnight bag in hand.

"Ya knows we needed to leave fifteen minutes ago," Uncle Jimmy scolded his wife.

"Hush yur mouth. I wasn't ready then, but now I is, so quit your yappin' and get in the car," Aunt Shirley snapped back. Tsu ran up to the vehicle before they could pull off.

"Do you think you guys could drop me off in town?" she asked adoringly. Uncle Jimmy and Aunt Shirley were well aware of her intentions. The entire Green Hill community had become privy to the delicate situation, and they were not too happy with it.

"You goin' to go see that boy, aren't cha?" Aunt Shirley insisted. Shaking her head at her niece the fool.

"All of Green Hill's talkin' bout you two." Uncle Jimmy informed her.

"Uncle Jimmy, please? Green Hill's got nothing to do with us."

"That's the most ignant thang I've ever heard, gal. When white folks don't like somethin' wit one colored, entire colored communities suffer. Ya best be more mindful, but I already knows ya don't know whatcha doin'." Uncle Jimmy contemplated for a few seconds. "Get in, Tsu." She hopped into the back seat of the car next to Lily's smiling face.

"Whys it gotta be a white man, Tsu?" asked Aunt Shirley, as they headed out of their driveway. Uncle Jimmy cut his eyes at his wife at her remark. Looking at Tsu's face in the rearview mirror, he felt compelled to explain it to Tsu in a better manner.

"It's not dat we dislike Paul, in fact we're really ratha fond of the boy. But, yur gettin' yurself so involved and vested in somethin' that can't really amount to nuthin'. Folks are real funny Tsu and don't take kindly to persons who don't stay in their places, colored or not colored, but specially those colored," explained Uncle Jimmy.

"We'll be really careful, Uncle Jimmy. Paul promised to have me back very early, before anyone notices I was there."

"He loves her, daddy. He'll make sure nothing happens to her," Lily offered.

"Hush yur mouth, gal. Ya don't know the first thing bout love." Aunt Shirley scolded Lily. "And white men don't go round fallin' in love with coloreds, Tsu. Ya just fixin' to get yur heart broken, if that's what yur thinkin'," Aunt Shirley crudely informed her.

"Too late for that. Tsu's so far on cloud nine, that the only way down is to shoot her outta the sky." Lily giggled.

"Lily, shush!" Even though Lily was trying to defend them, Tsu did not want her to disclose any more details of her personal feelings or her relationship with Paul to her aunt and uncle. "I know you guys are just concerned for me and I appreciate it, but the summer is almost over. I'll be going home soon and no matter what happens, this has been the greatest time of my life." Tsu attempted to appeal to their better natures.

"Hmm. Spoken like a real idiot, who's neva had her heart torn out of her chest. This will make time numba two fo ya, if I'm countin' correctly. I won't botha sayin' toldja so, when he ups and leaves ya fo' one of his own. Or betta yet, maybe he'll offer ya a job as the maid in his house. Ya can be his mistress when the red head turns him away at night." Tsu's sweet face saddened in the reflection of the rearview mirror.

"That's enuf, Shirley. Paul's not like that at'all and Tsu is betta than that. Give the gal more credit, meanie." He peered back into the rearview mirror, finding Tsu's worrisome face. "Don't lisen to nuthin' yur aunt says. If ya think its love, I'll take care of Green Hill and blabba mouth ova there." Uncle Jimmy was still worried about the situation, but he wanted to offer his support to Tsu. They pulled up at the post office and Tsu climbed out of the vehicle.

"Thank you, Uncle Jimmy. I'll see you all tomorrow night." She kissed each of them and sent them on their way, before taking a seat on the curb. While waiting for Paul to arrive, she twirled the end of her braid. She pondered some of the things her aunt had suggested about Paul's intentions. They were troublesome to think about. Tsu also began to imagine what the night would be like, with him in his house. Just then an old truck pulled up to her.

"Can I offer you a ride Miss?" Her Adonis had arrived.

Chapter Ten

Paul and Tsu pulled up on a quaint green bungalow styled home just after dusk. Stars streaked across the sapphire sky, hovering against the backdrop of the landscape. In the front yard stood two mature Weeping Willows and a medium sized old, yellow dog. It was laid out across the front lawn. As they climbed out of the black Chevy truck, the dog rose to his feet and trotted over to greet Paul and to meet Tsu. Paul knelt over to scratch behind his loyal dog's ears.

"And who might this faithful companion be?" she inquired.

"This mangy mutt is called Lysander," Paul commented.

"From A *Midsummer's Night Dream?*" she asked and Paul nodded in agreement.

"I know it quite well," Tsu informed him, with a boastful look upon her face.

"I'm sure you do." He took hold of her hand, pulled it to his mouth and kissed the back of it softly. He nodded towards the front door of his home, past the front porch. "Let's get you inside before we come across any nosey little busy-bodies. I'd like to have you all to myself for a while, before we have to get back into the real world," Paul explained.

Unexpectedly, he scooped her up, climbed the steps of the wooden porch pushing through the evergreen door and carried her over the threshold into his home. He placed her down in the center entrance of his living room. She took a slow scan of the room. It was the first time she had been privy to his world. Up until now, they had spent all of their time in hers. She felt privileged to see where Paul had come from and to have access to his domain.

"Make yourself at home, Tsu. I'll just go grab us something cold to drink," Paul said heading towards his kitchen.

Inside was amazingly tidy for a bachelor. Cluttered but clean. Pictures of the Morrison family and Paul as a child, covered just about every wall in the living room. The mantle was shrouded with old sport trophies, wore-in mitts much too small for any adult, along with some very poorly crafted pieces of art work. Tsu lowered her brow as she picked up what appeared to be a lopsided clay colored pot. She didn't quite understand what it was supposed to be. Paul re-entered the room carrying two glass Coca Cola bottles. He immediately noticed the expression on her face.

"What?" he arrogantly inquired. "Gammy thought everything I did was….exceptional. Like all grandmothers should," he contested.

"Is that a fact, Mr. Morrison?" she jested. Placing the small pot back down on the mantle, she gave him a big smile. He handed her over a bottle of Coke.

"Come with me, Tsu. I'd like to show you something in the kitchen." He extended his hand to her.

"I've already told you that I don't know my way around a kitchen very well. Are you sure you want me in there? You've tasted my work." She expressed with a funny grimace on her face. Paul laughed at her remark.

"I won't let you mess up things too bad in there, promise." He crossed his index finger across his heart.

At Paul's request, Tsu curiously followed him into the kitchen, which had a soft glow exuding from it. Stepping through the doorway, Tsu saw a white frosted, round cake with candles all alit atop of it. Wrapping his arms around her small waist from behind, he whispered into her ear.

"Happy Birthday, Tsunami." He placed a kiss upon her bare shoulder. Stunned, she responded.

"But how did you know?" She turned around to face him, still remaining in his grasp.

"Lily told me. She keeps me pretty well informed of everything I need to know, Tsu. I know that your birthday is actually tomorrow, but I wasn't about to miss the chance to celebrate the day you were born now, was I?" he shared, flashing his sly, confident smile. They both walked over to the cake. "Make a wish!" He told her.

"What else could I possibly ask for?" she teased. Her humble playfulness warmed his heart.

"There's gotta be something else you want," he suggested. She looked down to the ground and then back up at him.

"All I want is you," she replied. He snickered.

"You already have me," he stated. Her statement brought relief to him though. "Go on. Make a wish. Anything you want." She rolled her eyes up to the corners of her sockets and thought for a moment. She knelt before the cake and bashfully grinned at him, before blowing out the candles. "Now don't tell me, cause it might not come true. Okay?"

"Cross my heart," she retorted, mirroring his gesture from earlier, crossing across her full breast.

"That's my girl." Paul picked up a large carving knife next to the cake and cut her a large piece. Tsu sank her teeth into the richness of the cake. It was delicious.

"Did you make this?" she asked. It confused her how he had the time to do so, as she stuffed her face full with her piece.

"Of course I did, Tsu. You keep forgetting that I was a little boy living with an old woman," he reminded her. "I can also darn my own socks and crochet granny squares." His confession made Tsu laugh. He cut himself a piece of cake and bit into it. "It is good though, isn't it? Just the right amount of Crisco I'd say."

"Crisco's one of my favorite soap ingredients," she retorted. They had become really good at making each other laugh. Tsu took some of the frosting on her fingers and slowly wiped it across Paul's face. He took her fingers into his mouth and began sucking them clean.

"Yum, seconds," he responded. He then began smearing his own frosted covered fingers onto her face in return. Backing her up against his refrigerator, he rubbed his frosted coated nose against hers. She tugged at his t-shirt, finding his bare stomach. He took hold of her hands and removed then from his abdomen. The action perplexed her. "At some point, I mean to have you in this kitchen, but not before the bedroom. You deserve to be treated to a proper bed first." He took her bottom lip into his mouth and sucked any remaining frosting from it. "Let's finish our cake and get cleaned up beforehand though." The way he considered her, made her feel more important to him. Even if a proper bed would only be for the night.

~   ~   ~   ~   ~

After they finished eating, they started cleaning up in the kitchen. It was lovely being there with him and working beside him. Something she could get used to, though she wouldn't dare expect it. They both knew the summer was coming to an end, and that she would be returning to Connecticut in a matter of weeks. She thought that it was best just to enjoy the time she had left with him, and to deal with leaving once the time came. While wiping frosting off of the refrigerator door, Tsu noticed a picture displayed on it. It resembled much younger versions of Paul and William in their high school baseball gear. She advanced closer to the photo, to get a better look. She had forgotten that she was told they were best friends. They looked very close.

"Does William come over often?" Tsu asked. Paul looked up from washing the last dish, and noticed her studying the photo on the fridge.

"Nah. My grandmother kept bees in the backyard and harvested honey from them." He walked closer to her while drying his hands with a damp towel. "Willy got stung here once and almost died. He's allergic to bees, so he hardly comes past the curb anymore."

"You keep bees too?" Tsu inquired with amazement in her voice. Paul chuckled.

"No, but the hives are still outback. Mrs. Calhoun comes over now and again to harvest the honey and the combs." He tossed the used towel back on the counter and took hold of Tsu's waist. "If there is a good amount left over, she even leaves some behind in a few jars for me, so I can make sweets for pretty girls such as yourself." He flirtatiously licked his lips.

"Girls, plural huh? And are there many of us girls, who are fortunate enough to be bestowed with such treats?" Tsu became slightly jealous by his comment and her face told him so.

"There's only one at the moment who has capture my most special attention, and that is worthy enough of such treats. Along with my many, many other talents," he flirtatiously reassured her.

"Is that so, Mr. Morrison?" Seeing Paul being so flirtations was arousing to Tsu and she wanted to be nearer to him, even if he were trying to make her jealous. Her eyes dropped to his torso. Observing where her focus had become drawn too, Paul distracted her with a simple statement.

"I like having you in my home, Tsu." It was a genuine statement.

"I'm enjoying being here with you as well, Paul," she said. "But, I have a confession." Paul's eyes widened. She inched closer to him, as if she were about to reveal some devastating secret. In just

139

above a whisper she said, "I forgot to bring my night clothes." Paul laughed in amusement.

"The horror!" He teased. "You can grab one of my T-shirts out of the top drawer in the back bedroom." He directed her down the long hallway. "It's the last door on the left." Paul continued to clean up the mess on the table from the cake, as Tsu left the kitchen.

~   ~   ~   ~   ~

Once she made her way to the room, Tsu flicked on the bedroom light switch. His room was pretty plain, but it was cozy. Just a bed, one nightstand with an overly read Bible and Shakespeare's *The Tempest* on it and a tall wooden dresser. Opening the top drawer, she pulled out a white T-shirt, closed her eyes and inhaled. Would she ever get tired of his smell? When she opened her eyes, she spotted a small white box in the front corner of the open drawer. Her curiosity got the better of her and she opened it. It was a diamond and gold ring. The ring and the box looked too new to have had belonged to anyone beforehand. And by the look of it, it didn't appear to be what she thought was Paul's taste. But maybe she didn't really know what his taste was like. Tsu hadn't realized that Paul had made his way to the bedroom doorway, and was staring at her. He was petrified.

Paul had forgotten about the damn thing and he feared confusing Tsu. He nervously began pushing his hair back out of his face, and immediately began blurting out an explanation.

"The day you came into town, I was there picking up that ring." He let out a sigh. "I fully intended on giving it to Megan at the Fourth of July picnic. I'm sure it was expected, as our relationship had become so predictable. It was the only logical next step." He approached Tsu, as she continued to hold the tiny white box in her hand. "Then you happened. I met you, and everything changed for me and it's been in there ever since, I swear. I couldn't even think about marrying her after I met you in the street that day. Honest to Goodness, Tsu," he promised. "Something was always missing there. That something was you, Tsu. When I touched you that day and every day since, my world has been changing." He looked desperately into hers eyes. It was evident that the ring meant for Megan, had put a damper on the mood and possibly the evening. He hoped that it wouldn't be so.

Tsu placed the small white box back into its place in the corner of the drawer. Walking into him she pushed herself onto her toes to give Paul a kiss. She held him in her arms and it was reassuring to him, that she believed him. She didn't want to think about Paul marrying Megan, but she didn't like that he still had the ring for meant for Megan in his possession. Perhaps he would be able to put it to use once Tsu left town. Or maybe he had other intentions. Her aunt's words from earlier in the evening came to her mind. The statement about Paul marrying Megan and keeping Tsu around as his mistress when his wife turned him away. Was she his concubine in training? Her thoughts were interrupted.

"You haven't even changed yet," he inspected.

"No, not yet. I found your shirts, but I didn't get the chance to."

"I'll just go let in and feed Lysander. I'll be back in a jiffy." Paul kissed her once more and proceeded out of his bedroom. She didn't know how she should feel. Jealous and envious felt like the appropriate emotions, but did she have the right? She had given herself to him freely and had asked nor expected anything in return from him. But, she had no intentions of staying behind to play his mistress. She would go home before conceding to that type of an existence. However, she believed that he did have an authentic affection for her. She didn't feel like he was taking advantage of her during their summer romance. Their time together was slowly dwindling and she wanted to savor every last moment of it. Tsu noticed a silver pair of scissors on top of the dresser. She decided to cut the collar off of the T-shirt before putting it on. She knew how much Paul liked having access to her collar bone. Also she didn't want either one of them to be thinking about Megan O'Shea anymore.

~   ~   ~   ~   ~

When Paul returned to the bedroom, Tsu was seated in a straddled position atop the bed. Her braid was undone and her hair was crinkled to one side. She was wearing nothing but what use to look like one on his old shirts. Tsu had cut off so much of the collar that both her shoulders were completely exposed to him. In fact, the only thing keeping the shirt up and on, was that it was caught and clinging to her ample breast. She looked incredible to Paul. Scantily dressed. Her hair in disarray. He stripped out of his clothes while taking the sight of her in. He wanted her intensely and couldn't wait to ravage her over and over again in his bed. He no longer needed to be so careful or so controlled with her. Tsu had become quite accustomed to him at this point. She even experienced great pleasure when he was able to be a bit more vigorous with her. Paul climbed his naked body onto his bed and brought both he and Tsu to ecstasy several times that night.

~   ~   ~   ~   ~

In the morning, Tsu continued wearing only the cut up white t-shirt, while they made and ate breakfast together in the kitchen. Paul wore only his pajama bottoms. He kept true to his word, and he had indeed enjoyed having her in his kitchen in the earlier hours of the morning before their breakfast. Still, he couldn't resist taking in eyefuls of her delectable body while they ate. She noticed and liked him doing so.

"After breakfast I'd like to take you on a drive before I bring you home. If that would be alright with you, that is?"

"That would be lovely, Paul. I'm really not looking forward to stepping back into the real world yet, either," Tsu admitted. "This summer's been like a dream, I'm not sure if I'm ready to wake up from.

"I can share your sentiment. But inevitably we all must wake up, whether dreams are realized or not."

"Unfortunately, you are correct, Paul," she responded. She understood his message, but she couldn't rightly say she understood what he meant by it.

"If we're gonna get going, we gotta get outta here soon. People will be out and about and on their way to church before we know it."

"Alright. I'm more tired than hungry anyways."

"Me too." Paul laughed. They had been up for most of the night.

They quickly finished the bites of food in their mouths, as they were anxious to get out of town for a while. Tsu put on the same clothes she had worn from the night before. She had forgotten to bring any extra clothing with her at all.

"It'll have to do", she told herself.

~   ~   ~   ~   ~

On the front porch, Mrs. Calhoun was getting an eyeful herself. She watched Paul through his front windows, fraternizing with the colored girl. Neither one of them had noticed the older woman that had been gawking at them, for most of the morning in the corner windows. Inside, they both continued to prepare themselves for their trip. Once they were ready, Paul peered out of the small windows of the front door. He wanted to make sure the street was clear for him and Tsu to leave.

"The coast looks clear. Will make a quick dash to the truck. Just keep your head down until we get out of the center of town, okay?"

"Alright. It's funny acting like what we're doing is wrong." He took hold of her slender shoulders.

"Nothing we're doing is wrong." He stroked the side of her sun-kissed face. "People just have mixed up opinions is all, Tsu." He took hold of her hand. "You ready?"

"Ready!"

As they stepped out the front door, they collided into Mrs. Calhoun's scrutinizing stare. Tsu immediately let go of Paul's hand and turned her eyes to the aged wooden panels of the front porch.

"Why Paul, if your grandmother could see you carryin' on in such a manner with a nigger, and in her house," Mrs. Calhoun scolded. The words and interaction offended Tsu, but it also reminded her of her place. She knew she didn't have the right to be there with Paul, in town. Paul grabbed Tsu's hand once again. He felt compelled to protect her against the world as he knew it. He was honored to stand beside her, which gave Tsu the courage to stand proudly beside him as well.

"I believe my grandmother would be delighted that I was happy for a change, Mrs. Calhoun. And I would appreciate it if you wouldn't refer to the love of my life with such vulgarity, or you will no longer be welcomed here. In my home, Mrs. Calhoun," he sternly stated. "Is that understood, ma'am? Come on, Tsu." Paul didn't even give her the opportunity to respond to him. They pushed passed Mrs. Calhoun, whose jaw was practically dragging on the porch as they drove off.

Shocked and appalled by the way Paul Morrison had spoken to her, Mrs. Calhoun marched herself over to her burgundy Chrysler. She promptly headed over to the church to attend Sunday Service. All the Lexingtonians needed to know about this.

~   ~   ~   ~   ~

Paul was unusually quiet, not saying much of anything during the ride. Except for disclosing that they were going someplace where they wouldn't be bothered. He sat soundlessly next to her in the truck. It was pretty obvious that Paul was upset by the morning's events on his front porch. Tsu was uncertain how she was supposed to feel once again. On the one hand, he had just confessed that she was the love of his life. And to a prominent member of society. But now, he was in such an agitated state, that Tsu did not recognize his demeanor.

Internally Paul was trying to process and figure out his next move. He knew that Mrs. Calhoun was the biggest gossip in town. For sure the news of he and Tsu would spread through Lexington like a wildfire before the days end. After a short drive through the country, Paul pulled over into a grassy knoll. Taking Tsu's hand and guiding her through his door, they walked towards an open meadow with a small babbling brook off ahead in the distance.

"I like to come here sometimes to think," he said, sounding less tensed than he actually looked. He let go of her hand and walked a few steps away from her, kneeling beside the brook.

"It's beautiful here." Tsu thought it was peaceful enough and if it would help him get back into the good mood that he was in prior to Mrs. Calhoun's intrusion, she would love it. "Is everything alright, Paul?" Tsu asked knowing that Paul appeared to be anything other than alright. Paul walked over to Tsu and reached for her hand.

"I'm sorry you had to go through that this morning, Tsu. I don't think that Lexington will be a place that you and I will be able to exist in, Tsu. Actually I'm fairly sure we can't be together here anymore," he confessed.

Tsu became alarmed. She was uncertain of what Paul was getting ready to disclose to her. Is this the moment, she thought. Is this the moment where he tells me that all that we've had is over? She wasn't emotionally prepared for the trice. She thought they had a couple more weeks left. Her heart jumped up into her throat and she couldn't speak, waiting for him to drop the bomb on her. The pain of it choked her up.

"The school year starts for me in a couple of days, but I've been looking into other school positions and found an opportunity in Philadelphia for September. I think that will be a better place for us, Tsu. We won't have to hide as we have been. Still won't be easy, but we can be out in the open," he confided to her. This was completely

147

unexpected and Tsu couldn't believe what he was suggesting. "Will you go to Philadelphia with me?"

Still choked up, Tsu's only response was mouthing the letters O K. She couldn't believe that he was willing to leave his life behind, to start a new one with or for her. Opening her balled up hand, he placed a small silver ring into her palm.

"This belonged to my mother. Once upon a time, a modest carpenter gave this ring to a simple school teacher. That school teacher told me that when I found my split-apart...soul mate, that this ring signified true love, without any illusions of grandeur. And that that love would be protected and bound together by the strength of something purer than precious metals. That it would be supported by divine intervention. I think she would've wanted me to give it to you." Tsu stood in disbelief and Paul gently kissed her. "I think I've loved you all my life, Tsunami."

Chapter Eleven

Upon returning Tsu to her family's home early Sunday evening, Paul was conflicted with both feelings of happiness and fear. He attempted to mask his fear behind meager, unconvincing smiles. The two of them had studied each other's expressions well over the past several week, so Tsu could tell that he was troubled. Even though they had just had the most remarkable twenty-four hours, and to top it off she was now wearing his mother's ring

"Paul, your mood is worrying me. We've had such an amazing day, but you hardly seem happy." She considered for a moment if he was just trying to be a good guy, because of what happen on his porch. "You don't have to go through with....solidifying our relationship to try to prove that you're a decent guy to anyone, or me." Tsu wanted to console him, but mostly to offer him a way out. She presumed that he felt obligated to ask for her hand. Even though he hadn't technically asked for it. Paul was outraged by Tsu's statement. He hastily punched the dashboard of his truck in the Gaines' driveway. The action startled Tsu. She had never seem him angry before. Especially not with her.

"How could you think that? Have I led you to believe in some way that I want anything less than you, every day of my life? For the rest of our lives?" he responded adoringly, but he was upset with her for implying that he wasn't completely invested in her. "I gave you my mother's ring because you have captured me mind, body and soul and I want to build my life with you. I knew for certain that you were my one, after that kiss on the field house. I had every intention of proposing to you before Mrs. Calhoun's visit this morning. Why do you think I had the ring on me?" He took a deep breath in, pushed his hair from his face and appeared to be calmer. Tsu continued to listen to his declaration. "Why don't you know what you are and what you mean?" He caressed her face. "Everything I've done over the past few weeks has been for you, to be with you. You've inspire me and I'm better because of it." He hesitated searching for the words to explain his disposition for the day. "Tsu, I'd be lying if I told you I wasn't worried. Now that we're back in Lexington and we've been found out, the fairytale is over. I've lived in this town for a long time and I know these people well. They'll never accept us. Believe me, September can't come soon enough," Paul revealed his fear to her. It was not from being trapped with her liked she assumed. He was afraid of the racism and what the townspeople would do to her. They both climbed out of his truck and made their way over to the front steps.

"How bad is it gonna be?" she asked.

"Mrs. Calhoun can destroy anyone in town and she is the biggest bigot I know, Tsu. By now, she'll have the whole town riled up. Thankfully she doesn't know who you are. That's gonna buy us some time."

"Maybe you can speak with her or apologize." Paul's face tensed at her. Surely she didn't expect that that was something he would actually consider doing.

"I wasn't about to let her disrespect you then and I not gonna stand for it now, Tsu." He stroked the side of her face. "I cherish you and I'll cherish you all the days of my life, if you let me. Don't ask me to apologize for that." He kissed the back of her hand, now the proud owner of his mother's ring and pulled her into his arms. "Trust me. I'll never let anyone hurt you."

Just then, Aunt Shirley, Lily and Uncle Jimmy pulled up, observing the two love stricken fools embracing. Paul didn't let Tsu out of his arms, as the family removed themselves from their vehicle. Her aunt and uncle, disapprovingly viewing the sight of them. Lily flew out of the car and ran over to Paul.

"Paul!" She yelled, jumping into his arms. "Did you bring me anything?" She looked so charming. Aunt Shirley didn't say a word to either one of them, and continued on into her house. She flashed Paul a sharp look as she entered her home.

"As a matter of fact...," his voice trailed off and he reached into his shirt pocket, revealing the diamond and gold ring from his dresser drawer. He slid the two sizes too big band around her tiny ring finger. Lily's eyes lit up.

"Thank you, Paul." She hugged him and ran off into the house to show her mother what she had been given. Tsu looked to Paul, waiting for an explanation.

"What?" he questioned. "She's partly responsible for our union, don'tcha think? It's the least I could do," he rambled. His expression changed and he looked worrisome once again. "I should get home now, Tsu."

"You can't stay a little longer?"

"I wish I could. School starts in a few days and I'm not sure what I'm going home too."

"I don't want you to go, if you're going to be in danger, Paul." His comment worried her. He scoffed, hoping to dismiss any fearful thoughts she was having.

"I'll be fine. I'll come by tomorrow to check on you. I want you to avoid town though. At least until we can leave, promise?" Tsu nodded in agreement and he kissed her sweetly on the lips in front of Uncle Jimmy, who had been sternly overlooking the two of them. "Excuse me, sir, can I have a word with you?" Paul requested, and the two men walked a few steps away from Tsu. "Mr. Gaines, I'm sorry for all the trouble I'm about to cause you sir, but Mrs. Calhoun came to my house this morning and saw me with Tsu."

"Damn it, Paul. Dat woman spreads good news fasta than Christians can spread the good word. I thought ya two were gonna be careful?" Uncle Jimmy gestured towards Tsu. Paul quickly re-directed Jimmy's attentions back on himself.

"It's all my fault, sir. But never-mind that. I'm sure the whole town knows by now and they are fixin' to retaliate in some way. Luckily not many people know who Tsu is, so I need you to keep her out of town til I can arrange for us to leave."

"Leave? Where ya leavin' too?" asked Jimmy.

"I found a job in Philadelphia, sir. It starts in a couple of weeks, but I still need to finalize our living situation. The sooner we get outta here, the better for Green Hill and your family," Paul explained.

"We'll keep her here, but ya best be movin' quick. White folks won't hold off too long. Pardon my expression, Paul," Uncle Jimmy exclaimed. He felt embarrassed and excused himself because of Paul's skin color.

"Believe me, I understand, Mr. Gaines." The two men shook hands and Uncle Jimmy headed over to his house as Paul made his way to his Chevy truck.

"Mr. Gaines?" Uncle Jimmy turned back to see what Paul wanted. "Take good care of my future wife for me." Paul called out before jumping into his truck and pulling out of the dirt driveway.

"Future wife?" Uncle Jimmy questioned. "Tsunami! You got some splainin' to do, gal," he commanded, walking her into the house with him.

~   ~   ~   ~   ~

Days passed slowly, and Paul sat in his empty classroom the first day of school. The young students were boycotting his class, most likely directed by their parents. They made sure to give him a welcome Paul wouldn't forget though. 'Nigger Lover Go Home', stretched across his chalkboard. Paul was determined not to be beaten. He simply erased the board and sat in seclusion in his classroom for the remainder of the day. However, seeing the message only reminded him of his homecoming after dropping Tsu off Sunday night.

~   ~   ~   ~   ~

When Paul arrived at his house, the front windows were smashed in. After searching the living room covered with broken glass, he found the bricks that had been thrown through them. 'Nigger Lover' had been written on each of them.

"Cowards! Could've waited until I was home," Paul sounded.

He knew there would be some turmoil, but in no way could he have imagined the extent of his town's hatred. These were the very people he knew most of his life and interacted with on a daily basis. In his years living there, he had witnessed many injustices towards the coloreds in town. Unfair treatment, boycotts, cross burnings and color men disappearing from town, suspected to have been murdered. Whites that had stood up for or besides the coloreds were treated less harshly. Still, Paul had seen white men beat and run out of town for doing such. He expected the latter to be his punishment as well. He continued to search the house for any other damage, but found nothing of consequence. Out of the corner of his eye, he caught a glimpse of some fiery flames burning in the backyard. It looked like the beehives were set on fire. He hastily ran into the kitchen to fill up a mop bucket with water. Upon running through the back door to investigate, he collided into Lysander's hanging body. The dog had been beaten, stabbed and strung up in a large Maple tree in the backyard.

"No! Lysander boy, I'm so sorry. What they do to ya, boy? What did they do?" Panicked, he sawed furiously at the bristles of the rope with his pocket knife, until the lifeless dog collapsed into his lap. Tears bombarded his eyes. "Come on boy," he called out, half expecting Lysander to respond, but the bloodied dog never did. He had been left there, hanging for hours as a message for Paul when he returned home. Paul sat rocking his faithful companion back and forth in the yard, as the hives smoldered behind them. "I'm so sorry I wasn't here. I didn't know, boy. I'm so fucking sorry!" He cried out, holding Lysander to his chest. "Can you ever forgive me?" He sat there weeping, holding his dearly departed dog in his lap, until the last of the flames died out. The smell of burnt honey permeated the air. Paul's tears had run dry on his face, which was now streaked with a mixture of dirt and Lysander's blood. If his fellow Lexingtonians were capable of this, what would they do once they redirected their attentions on Tsu? He knew that he would be putting her and the Gaines in jeopardy, if he persisted with his visitations.

~ ~ ~ ~ ~

Filled with anger and grief, Paul dutifully managed to do the just and right thing. Once he was able to pull himself together, he reported the incidence to the local authorities. The operator informed him that they would send an officer over promptly. It took almost an hour after that call, for anyone to show. The fiftyish, smug, Sheriff R.T. Bingham arrived at the scene.

"Glad you could finally make it here, Sheriff," Paul sarcastically bellowed out. He already had a few beers under his belt as he waited for the sheriff to show. The alcohol along with his anger made him a bit loose with his tone. "Some folks have vandalized my home and murdered my dog."

"Is that a fact, son?" Sheriff Bingham coolly asked. Paul nodded in support of his statement.

"When I got home this evening, the living room windows were shattered and I found Lysander, bloody and hanging from a tree out back." Paul tried to keep his cool, but he suspected that the Sheriff was already aware of what had happened. Sheriff Bingham was the worst kind of racist. He had many unjust and inhumane crimes under his belt as the law in town.

"Is that right, son? Do you have any idear who might wanna do something like this to ya, son?" Sheriff Bingham condescendingly asked.

"I can't say any one person in particular Sheriff, that's why I called you here. To investigate," Paul snapped.

"Don't get smart with me, boy." Pronouncing each word, Sheriff Bingham drove his index finger into Paul's chest. He didn't appreciate Paul's tone. "It looks like you mighta pissed someone off. Can ya think bout somethin' ya mighta done that would make someone angry witcha, boy?"

"Nothing of anyone's concern, Sheriff," Paul sternly stated.

"Is that so?" Sheriff Bingham reached down to pick up a brick and read the script off of it.

"Nigger Lova. Why would anyone write somethin' like that?" the Sheriff questioned.

"Probably because this town's filled with narrow minded assholes and nosey little busy bodies, who think they have the right to get involved in other people's private affairs, sir." Paul was losing his patience with the sheriff. Bingham scoffed at his impetuousness.

"Ya think so, huh?" The Sheriff looked quizzically at Paul. "Well, son, there ain't much we can do bout broken windas and dead dogs. I suggest ya bury the dog, sweep up the glass and keep yur distance from that nigger gal of yurs." This was the first time that the sheriff eluded to knowing anything about Tsu. "These types of things have a way of escalatin' to people, quickly if ya catch my drift, son." It sounded like a threat to Paul.

"Loud and clear, Sheriff." Paul understood what the sheriff meant, and he knew he would not be able to keep his cool much longer with Bingham. "Thanks for the advice. You can show yourself out, right?" Sheriff Bingham flashed Paul a crooked smile before leaving the premises.

~   ~   ~   ~   ~

Paul buried Lysander under the Maple tree he had been hung from and made him a headstone out of rocks. Afterwards, he entered the house swept up the scattered glass and boarded up the broken windows. Considering what the sheriff had said, he decided that it would be safer for Tsu if he kept his distance. At least until after the move. His main focus needed to be getting them to Philadelphia as soon as he possibly could. It wouldn't be easy for him to stay away from Tsu, but he had to do what was best for everyone involved.

~ ~ ~ ~ ~

The bell rang signaling the end of the school day, pulling him back from his memory. Paul packed up his brown leather satchel and a small box with a few of his personal items from his classroom. He marched to the main office and handed the secretary his letter of resignation. There were a few other teachers there, along with the administrative staff. No one said a word to him. The whole day had been spent in silence and seclusion. He had been shunned.

"It's been a real pleasure working with such fine upstanding Christians such as yourselves," he stated. They did not appreciate his snide comment, but still not a word was said to him. He headed straight home and continued packing up his old life into cardboard boxes. He was saving the window repair for last. He didn't want to go through all the trouble of replacing the glass, just so they could come back and smash them again, just despite him. He put up a for sale sign in the front yard. He hoped that it would be enough of a signal to the town that they had won and that he was leaving. He had already plan to move beforehand, so what difference would it make it if he let them believe that they had chased him out.

~   ~   ~   ~   ~

Meanwhile, Green Hill did not appreciate all the attention brought upon them because of Tsu and Paul's relationship. Even if the white community didn't know which colored girl Paul was involved with, the Green Hill residents were already in the know. Paul's truck had been seen outside the Gaines' on several occasions. The neighbors were beginning to speculate why he had suddenly taken an interest in the Gaines', especially while Jimmy was at work. It was assumed that Jimmy's relatively attractive niece, had caught Paul's attention.

~   ~   ~   ~   ~

Outside of the Gaines' home, a gathering of angry colored neighbors came to voice their concerns over all the trouble being caused in Green Hill. Jimmy Gaines stood with several of his closest friends against the angry herd of gatherers outside his front door.

"What right they got bringin' down all dis trouble on us?" a colored women called out. Cheers in agreement sounded. "They don't want us, just her. Why we's gotsta pay for her. She a outsida." More cheers of agreement sounded amongst the crowd.

"They're in love!" Lily defensively cried out.

"Those crackers done set a cross on fire in front of Ray's yard. My daughtas are harassed on da way to school and Joe's wife done los' her cleanin' job. Fo' what? So anotha white man can have hisself a lil' brown tail. We don't think so, Jimmy," an angry neighbor explained. More cheers sounded in support.

"Lisen here!" Uncle Jimmy called out. "I knows we all are frustrated and upset, but, place da blame where it lies. It's Lexington. Not Tsu or Paul." Uncle Jimmy spoke with conviction. He wanted to persuade his neighbors to look at the real issue. "Now Paul's been a frien' ta all of us, when mos' white folks soona spit in our faces. He's axed us for a few days and we can give 'em dat.

"Why we gotta suffa for yur niece. She ain't one of us. She don't even live in Green Hill," another woman called out.

"She my kin, and I always take care of family. Like I take care of all of you and yur families," Uncle Jimmy reminded them. "Now I'm tellin' ya to keep yur eyes open, keep safe and Paul and Tsu both, will be gone in a few more days. Once they're gone, things will go back to normal. Is dat understood?" Uncle Jimmy was accustomed to being the authority figure in Green Hill. Besides his wife, occasionally, there was no one who would really challenge him. Not that they needed to, he was pretty fair in most matters.

"Alright, Jimmy. We'll give 'em a few more days. I sure as hell hopes yur right bout dat," the spokesman sounded. "But, I don't give a damn if they do love each otha if Green Hill's gonna burn for it. Know whatta mean?" The crowd and its elected spokesperson disperse, still sardonically chattering amongst themselves as they made their way off of Jimmy's property.

~   ~   ~   ~   ~

Paul made arrangements for he and Tsu to leave for Philadelphia by the week's end. Meanwhile, Tsu laid low as instructed by her Uncle Jimmy and at Paul's request. She even abandoned her soap making venture, as she was told that the townspeople had boycotted her product. Ever since the scandal broke out about her and Paul, no one was willing to buy her soap. It only took a few day for the town's people to find out that Tsu was Paul's girl. Megan finally spilled the beans. She was utterly embarrassed that Paul had claimed Tsu as the love of his life. She gave Tsu's name and the Gaines up to the town in order to hurt Paul, and hopefully the woman who had stolen him away from her.

~   ~   ~   ~   ~

With not much else to do, Tsu turned to her books to help pass the time. She begin to write to her mother, letting her know all that had happen to her since she came to Lexington. Lily entered the cozy little room to talk with Tsu, while she was writing.

"Golly, that mob was angry outside, but daddy fixed them," Lily gossiped.

"I heard everything." Tsu was saddened by the distress she was causing. "Everyone is so upset with us. Even Uncle Jimmy, though he hasn't said anything. I know he's displeased with me for putting you guys in this position."

"He's not mad." Lily hesitated for a moment, trying to think of the appropriate emotion. "I think he's afraid for you and Paul. Anywhere you two go, yur bound to encounter some kind of difficulty on account of you being colored and Paul being white." Lily hesitated once again. "I wish we were still making soap. Funny how you can miss a thing after only having it a little while."

"Me too, but Baker's customers aren't buying anymore, so there isn't much point in it anymore. After I'm gone and things settle down, maybe you can pick it up again," Tsu offered. Lily noticed that Tsu was writing a letter.

"Who's that for?"

"I'm writing to my mother. I'm telling her about all that has happened, thus far. She should be in New York by now, at Mrs. Ellington's townhouse." Tsu placed the letter in an envelope and sealed it shut. "I also put in that I will be going to Philadelphia with Paul and told her not to worry."

"Oh yeah, that reminds me. I saw Paul earlier by the lumber yard. He said to tell you he would stop by for a bit before dark." Tsu became agitated.

"Don't forget things like that, Lily. I haven't seen him in days and I miss him so much."

"I'm sorry." She felt bad for forgetting, but she had had so much on her mind, "Ima miss the both of you once you leave," Lily admitted.

"I know. Believe me, we're gonna miss you too," Tsu replied. "You've been such an important part of all of this." Lily threw her arms around Tsu and they held one another for a few seconds. "Help me pick out something to wear for later?" Tsu asked and Lily happily nodded in agreement.

~ ~ ~ ~ ~

Just after dusk, Paul pulled into the Gaines' driveway. Tsu had been impatiently sitting on the porch waiting for his arrival. He climbed out of his truck and headed over to greet her.

"Hey beautiful. I've missed seeing your face," Paul gently expressed, as he approached her.

"I've been so worried. I've missed you too." Tsu threw her arms around his neck and kissed him.

"I shouldn't stay long, but I wanted to fill you in on the plans." Paul sounded exhausted. "I found us an apartment, but it won't be ready 'til Monday. I figure we can leave early Sunday morning and be there by before nightfall. The professorship at the University I got, starts in two weeks, which will give us some time to get settled into our new place. I already submitted my syllabus, so we can focus on putting our first apartment together, *together*. "

163

Paul explained. They both smiled. It was obvious that he had been tiring himself out.

"You think of almost everything, but what am I supposed to do there?" Tsu flirtatiously inquired.

"Oh, that's the best part. The apartment I found has a small office in it, so you are going to write. You're pretty good at a few things Tsu, but I believe you were meant to be a writer," he commented.

"What if I were thinking of becoming a chef or a cook?"

"You're only gonna be allowed in the kitchen to eat meals. Those cookies you made, made a lasting impression on me, for life." He pulled her closer into him. "Besides, someone's gotta use the new oak desk and typewriter that'll be delivered on Monday."

"You do think of everything. But I will make my own decisions if you don't mind? Thank you very much. "

"Whatever you say, Tsunami." He held her close and breathed her in. "I best get going. Got lots of packing to finish up, if we wanna leave in a few days."

"Already? Will I see you before Sunday?" Tsu desperately inquired. Paul valued that she had missed him so.

"I'll try and come up with something." He gave her a wink before kissing the top of her head. "Lily!" he called out. "Where you at, beautiful? Don't let me leave without getting a hug from ya."

"Here I am." She ran up and jumped into his arms. Paul squeezed her.

"That's my girl." He set Lily down and kissed Tsu goodbye.

"Until next we meet," Tsu replied somberly.

"Until then." Paul climbed back into his truck, backed out of the driveway and headed home for the evening.

~   ~   ~   ~   ~

Saturday late afternoon, Lily retrieved a tiny white envelope from the mailbox with Tsu's name on it. She walked back into her house and into her room curiously regarding the letter. Tsu was in the middle of packing her things. Lily plopped herself down on her white bedspread.

"Tsu, there was a letter in the mailbox for you." She turned the envelope from back to front.

"From who?" Tsu inquired.

"Doesn't say. Just has yur name on it. Can I open it, for you?" Lily asked with excitement.

"No thank you. I can open my own mail." Tsu pulled the envelope from Lily's tight grip. She opened and read the single sentence on the card.

Meet me at the cabin tonight, after dark, for one last night!

"How romantic," Tsu sighed. The cabin reminded her of better times, before the town found out about them.

"What? What did the letter say?" Lily anxiously questioned.

"Paul wants to meet at the cabin tonight. One last time, before we leave tomorrow."

"He's so charmin'. Can I come? Please?" Lily pleaded with her eyes.

"I don't think so, Lily. Not this time." Tsu smiled at her, letting Lily know that she and Paul needed some alone time. Not wanting to get into any further discussions with her, Tsu walked away from her packing. She went into the kitchen to warm up the pre-made dinner Aunt Shirley had left in the icebox.

~   ~   ~   ~   ~

Tsu picked at the contents of her plate, waiting for time to pass by. She, Aunt Shirley and Lily made some casual small talk about Tsu's move for the following day. After dinner, she quickly put away the leftovers and cleaned up the kitchen. She changed into her green dress in the back bedroom for the evening. She set aside one other outfit on the bed for traveling. Blue knickers, a white sleeveless shirt and her tennis shoes.

"Are you leavin' now?" Lily asked.

"Leaving has a 'G' at the end of it. And yes, I am," Tsu responded.

"Dang it. I've gotten better though."

"Yes, you have. Much better. Just keep practicing and reading lots of books you love. Learning and knowledge is a wonderful thing, Lily. Remember that." Lily went over and hugged her.

"I'm gonna miss you so much, Tsu."

"I'm gonna miss you too. I'll be back a little later. Don't let Aunt Shirley know that I've left and don't tell your father," Tsu pleaded.

"I won't." They joined their pinkies together in a solemn promise. "Besides she's already gone down to the game to watch daddy. You think I can come visit you guys in Philadelphia sometime?" Lily inquired.

"Absolutely, Lily. But let's talk about it later, when I get back. I have to go. Paul's probably waiting for me right now." Tsu rushed the finishing touches of her appearance, pinching her cheeks to add color to them.

"Sure thing." Lily held back any further questions. She knew that Tsu was anxious to get to the cabin.

~   ~   ~   ~   ~

Tsu made her way through the woods, and when she stumbled upon the small cabin, she smiled. This place held so many fond memories for her from the summer, and she was going to miss the cabin most of all. She saw the warm orange glow projecting from the lantern inside. She immediately smiled again.

"Paul!" she sighed. She ran bursting through the front door with excitement. Tsu's eyes widened in shock and fear. It wasn't Paul waiting for her there.

It was William Baker.

Chapter Twelve

"Hello Tsu. I've been waiting for you all summer," William drawled, as he walked over to her. He struck her hard across her face, knocking her down to the ground. Her nose began to bleed. "Here, let me help you up." Tsu kicked at William as he tried to pull her off of the ground. She got him right in the lip. "You little bitch, whore." William pulled back his fist and popped Tsu in her face, knocking her to the ground once more. The room was spinning and she couldn't think clearly. She was barely able to focus or to lift her body off of the floor.

"Why are ya doing this?" she murmured, stalling for time and hoping to distract him from hitting her anymore. From the smell and the look of him, she could tell he was drunk. She recalled Paul telling her how unruly William could be when he had had a few to many.

William looked at his wounded prey and begun to become aroused by his handiwork. He stroked at his growing member in his pants. Tsu also remembered what Lily had told her, Tsu's first night in town. *William Baker fancied colored girls and liked to get rough with them.* Tsu's face looked horrified as she watched him touching himself. She could only imagine what he was going to do to her, and they were all terrible thoughts. She'd have to find a way to break free from him the first chance she got.

William thoroughly liked the look of Tsu beaten and bloodied by his hand. He continued to rub at his crotch as Tsu sank deeper into her fear beneath him.

"Relax, Tsunami. I'm not gonna have my way with you, just yet. Paul will be here soon, and then we can all have ourselves a real good time." William was quite agitated by all that had occurred while he was on his honeymoon. The idea that he had almost missed his opportunity to pay Paul back, infuriated him so much. He was insistent that the punishment needed to be much more severe for them now.

"You don't have to do this, William," Tsu pleaded. "Isn't Paul your friend? Your best friend?" she questioned.

"Fuck Paul!" he hollered, causing Tsu to jolt backwards. He lit and took a drag of a cigarette, and a sip from his flask. "Paul is and has always been inferior to me. An insignificant thorn in my side," he scoffed. "Just another pawn to be manipulated and discarded when I see fit." He took another pull and another sip. "If it wasn't for that colored boy interfering back in high school, I would've gotten rid of Paul a long time ago. He didn't know his place then and apparently, he is still struggling with it." He threw the cigarette butt to the cabin floor and stomped it out. "I loathe the bastard. Truth be told I've loathed him for some time, Tsu. But you, you were the final tipping point. I hadn't really realized how much hatred I had for him, until I saw the two of you at the field house and in this very cabin."

In the moment, she realized that he had been watching her and Paul all of this time. The cigarette butts that Lily found around the cabin were his. Tsu recalled. Things were starting to make sense to her.

"But why me? What do I have to do with any of it?"

"He knew I wanted you and he pursued you anyways, like he didn't already have enough. I practically gave him the world on a silver platter. Megan, clothes, money if he needed it. All he had to do was play by my rules, but look at the thanks I got." William approached Tsu desperately trying to appear in control, but the alcohol exasperated his anger. Tsu pushed back as far as she could go against the cabin wall. Inhaling her sweet scent he said, "The greedy bastard wouldn't keep his fucking hands off you." William ran his hand alongside her shoulder and all she could do was cry. "Will you touch me, like how you touch him, Tsu?"

Tsu was mortified at the thought of touching this man as tenderly as she did Paul, but she was afraid of what he might do if she did not comply with his request. She reached out to caress his beautiful face. He closed his eyes and for a moment, he was able to forget that she was with him against her will. The touch was comforting and he appreciated the way it felt. He moved his face in conjunction to her touch. As she continued, he slipped his hand under her green dress and slowly started to slide it up her inner leg. Tsu's eyes grew big and she panicked. She swatted at the intrusive hand on her body and pulled her dress back down, recovering her legs. It was a natural reflex. She trembled before him, knowing that her action upset him. He couldn't believe that she had had the audacity to hit him. Instantly, he gathered up both of her wrist in one

171

of his hands. He took out a silver plated pistol and pressed the cold weapon into Tsu's face hard, causing her a great deal of discomfort. She twisted her face from side to side, trying to relieve the pressure from the cool weapon being jammed onto her face.

"You see this gun, sweetheart?" He closed in on her and licked the side of her face, positioning himself beside her ear. "I'm gonna fuck you while Paul watches. Then I'm gonna shoot him, hang you and let Green Hill or the clan take the wrap for it. Just like all the other times. Someone else always takes the fall for what I do." He pushed away from her ear, in order to look into her eyes. "I'm the only one who will ever know the truth," William confessed. He drunkenly tossed the gun into the air, barely catching it by the barrel. He swiftly swung it across the side of her head with such force, that the butt of the gun knocked her out on impact.

~   ~   ~   ~   ~

Paul drove his jam-packed truck into the Gaines' driveway. He assumed that it would be alright if he parked at the Gaines' for the night. Even if Mr. or Mrs. Gaines made him sleep in his truck, he and Tsu would be able to get an early start in the morning. He was completely exhausted. All the packing he had done and the preparations he had made, had taken a lot out of him. Thankfully, their new place was fully furnished, so he was able to leave most of the bulky stuff behind. All of his grandmother's furniture was old anyways. He thought Tsu might prefer to pick out more modern fixtures of her own. Most of the women he knew seemed to like that sort of thing, even though Tsu wasn't like most women. Upon hearing Paul's truck pulling in, Lily ran outside to meet him.

"Whatcha doing here, Paul?" Lily look confused. Tsu had been gone for about a half hour by now.

"I'm here to see Tsu," he said, rubbing his hand across the top of her braids. He pulled a folded piece of paper from his back pocket. "You guys left me this note to meet her at the cabin. I just thought it would be easier to park here instead of at the creek. Especially since we'll be leaving in the morning." Paul wasn't quite sure why Lily was asking about what she and Tsu had obviously planned together. Surely Lily was in on it.

"She's gone." Lily shrugged her shoulders. "You sent her a note to meet you at the cabin?" Lily questioned. She handed Paul the card that Tsu had left behind. Paul's face went white. *William,* he thought. He recognized the handwriting immediately when he read the note. William must've taken more time to disguise the handwriting on his note, but why? What was he up to and how did he know about the cabin? Paul wished that he had addressed William weeks ago when he told him he would've. He underestimated how sadistic and ruthless William could actually be, but he didn't have time to regret that now.

"Damn it!" He pounded the hood of his truck, slightly denting it. The distress of the situation re-energized him. "Listen to me carefully, Lily. Where's your father?" he frantically demanded, grabbing her small shoulders.

"It's Saturday! He's at the ball field, playing baseball," she cried out. Paul was frightening her.

"Go get him and bring him to the cabin." Paul checked his pockets looking for his Swiss blade, but he was without it. It must've made its way into one of the boxes.

"But Tsu made me promise not to tell. She wasn't supposed to leave. She'll get in trouble," she confided.

"She's already in trouble, Lily. William's got her." Lily's eyes widened. She knew what William liked to do to colored girls. "Get a few of the other players to the cabin as well. I may need help dealing with William. Run as fast as you can Lily, Tsu's in danger." Lily took off as fast as her lanky legs could carry her towards the fields. Paul headed in the other direction, tearing through the wood as quickly as the adrenaline would carry him.

~   ~   ~   ~   ~

When Tsu opened her eyes, her head was throbbing and blood was trickling down the side of her face. She tried to move, but her hands and feet were bound to the cot, and her dress had been removed. *How long have I been out?* She wondered. She looked around trying to locate William. She found him sitting on one of the chairs, in front of the door. He looked deep in thought. The silver plated pistol was still in hand and he sipped whisky from his flask with the other hand. A pool of rope rested beside him. Was it to be the instrument of her death? Realizing she had come to, William

174

spoke to her. He was growing rather impatient waiting for Paul to arrive.

"Soon, Tsu, soon. Paul will be here shortly and you and I will finally have our time together. Then I can be done with the both of you," he sadly reported. To her, it almost sounded like he regretted this decision. "Truth be told. I don't really want you anymore. Everything about you is false for me, not like her." His eyes watered. "You're just the only way I can hurt Paul." It seemed as if he were conflicted with his choices, however, she felt it would do her no good to try and reason with him. His mind was made up, even if his plan did trouble him.

Tsu closed her eyes and began reciting the Lord's Prayer, secretly working the ropes around her wrist. She envisioned being able to alert or save Paul if she could. Most of all, she was determined not to be taken against her will again. Even if it cost her, her life.

~   ~   ~   ~   ~

Paul arrived at the cabin in haste. He cautiously peaked through a window to assess the situation. He found William sitting by the door leaning his chair against the wall, with a gun in his hand. The circumstances were much more severe than Paul had anticipated and he had no weapon of his own. He looked around the cabin more and found Tsu tied to one of the old cots. Her head and nose were bleeding. Her face, swollen, and she was only clothed in her under garments. Seeing Tsu in her current condition, brought forth a rage in Paul that he had never known. He was going to kill William for what he had done to her.

~   ~   ~   ~   ~

Paul walked quietly up to the front door and kicked it in with all of his might. The door swung open so fast, that it knocked William out of his chair. He was hit so hard, that he released the gun from his hand when he hit the floor. Paul grabbed William's shirt and threw punch after punch at his *friend*. William tried to fight back, but he had drank too much and Paul had the element of surprise working in his favor. William's face bloodied quickly.

"What the hell is wrong with you, Willy? Why are you such a sick fuck?" Paul yelled at William holding him to his face.

"I think therefore I can." William spat blood into Paul's face. "All that matters is what I want. Don't you know that by now?" William mumbled out through his bludgeoned mouth.

"I loved you, Willy, like a brother, always." His eyes began to well up. "Even with all your bullshit. Why would you do this to me?" Paul pleaded with him, trying to understand William's motives.

"Fuck you, Paul. You still don't get it. I'm incapable of loving you and I'm still gonna fuck her. First chance I get, brother," he cackled. Paul pulled William closer to his face until their noses were practically touching.

"You come near either of us or touch her ever again, Willy, and I will end you. You hear me?" Paul shouted into his face, and he tossed his barely responsive body to the side. He rushed over to Tsu and begun untying the ropes around her feet, as Tsu had already loosened the rope around her wrists. "Can you walk?" he asked making a careful assessment of her wounds and her body.

"It's just my head. Just a little dizzy. He was going to rape me while you watched, Paul, and then kill the both of us, you first and then let Green Hill or the clan take the fall for it. He said he has killed others and he already tried to kill you in high school, but that a colored boy got in the way," Tsu sobbed.

"What?" Paul sounded in disbelief.

"He said he loathed you always, and that I was going to be how he would make you pay, Paul."

"Listen, Tsu. Get out of the cabin and go wait for me by my truck. I gotta find his gun." Tsu hugged him before stumbling out the door towards the cliff. Every time they had met at the cabin, Paul parked across the creek. Naturally, she assumed that his truck was on the other side of the creek. Through the window, Paul saw that she was heading in the wrong direction. He quickly abandoned his mission to locate the gun and stood to his feet to go after her.

Just as Paul was about to run through the door and call after her, William grabbed his leg causing Paul to fall. He smashed his face onto the hard floor. The two of them rolled around the small cabin grappling, throwing blow after blow. William squeezed at Paul's larynx as Paul struggled to get free from him. He was able to pry

William's fingers from around his throat and kneed him in his rib cage. Scrambling to his feet, he gave William a swift kick to the face. More blood shot out of his mouth. Exhausted and barely able to catch his breath, Paul ran out of the cabin in search of Tsu.

William pulled himself together, retrieved his gun and chased after the two of them through the darkened woods. The two men quickly begun closing the gap on Tsu, one after the other. Paul could see her within his reach, and he was so thankful he had caught up to her. William only seconds behind him, had Paul in his line of sight and took aim with his gun.

"Paul!" He called out. Paul turned suddenly, at the sound of his name. In doing so, he tripped on a root protruding out of the dirt. William fired six rounds wildly though the woods, nearly missing Paul as he fell to the earth. While he was down, Paul saw Tsunami getting struck by at least one of the bullets. She was just about to make the jump off the cliff. He thought there was no way she had been able to clear the ledge.

"TSUNAMI!" Paul cried out. He made his way to the edge, but couldn't see her. He threw his body into the water, diving down search of hers. William made his way over to the edge, to see what he had done.

After emerging from the temped water, Paul pulled Tsu's body up to the surface so she could get air. She was still breathing but her head was cracked open even more. He knew for certain she had smashed it into the jagged, under water ledge below. Her shoulder was also profusely bleeding, but he couldn't tell how bad the damage was. Paul spotted William hovering up above, on the cliff. He was wiping his bloody face with his silk handkerchief.

"William? Please, help me? She may be dying," Paul begged.

"I hope that bitch does for all the torment and confusion she's caused me, like she could ever be...," he hesitated. "And you can follow her, friend," William called out. Paul regarded the man he thought of and called his best friend for so many years, in disbelief. They could both hear a mob of men, frantically searching the woods coming towards the cliff. William aimed the empty pistol at Paul, firing an imaginary shot at him, before disappearing from his sight.

Paul swam her unconscious body to shore. He carried her up the hillside and through the woods as fast as he could. All the while, urging her to wake up. Branches and bushes swatted his face and body as he charged through the forest. His hands were of no use to him, though he shielded her as much as he could against the assault. He needed to get her medical attention. On his way to his truck, he ran into Jimmy, Lily and several players from the baseball team.

"What happ'n? We heard gunshots!" Jimmy asked. Tearfully Paul replied.

"Willy had her, but I got her out. He shot at me and one of the bullets hit Tsu when she went to jump off the cliff. She didn't make the jump. She smashed her head on the ledge. She won't wake up." Uncle Jimmy regarded his lifeless niece and attempted to take her body from Paul, but he wouldn't let her got. *Not this time. I'm let letting go, this time.* Paul told himself.

"Here, let us help ya." Uncle Jimmy could see that he was fatigued, but he gathered pretty quickly that Paul would sooner die than Tsu could be pried from his protective arms. The men helped Paul carry Tsu's body as much as he would allow them to do, the remaining way. This time he was determined to see the life sacrificed for him, saved. Tsu meant everything to him.

"Where is William now?" Jimmy asked.

"I don't know. He may be headed to the fields by now," Paul responded.

"Don't worry, Paul, we knows these woods like the back of our hands. We'll find 'em. Dat boy's hurt far too many of our girls, dat its' bout time William Baker had hisself a accident," Uncle Jimmy explained to Paul. They reached Paul's truck and loaded her in. "Lily get in da house and lock up." She quickly did as she was instructed.

"I'm gonna take her to the colored hospital, Mr. Gaines," Paul stated. Uncle Jimmy started to turn away. "Jimmy?" Paul called out. Uncle Jimmy came back to the driver's side window. "Willy's allergic to bees."

Uncle Jimmy nodded at him and Paul peeled out of the driveway, glancing into the rear view mirror. He saw the men huddle around each other, than one by one scatter into the darkness. Paul couldn't worry about William anymore. His only concern had to be saving Tsu.

Chapter Thirteen

Three days had gone by in the hospital since the accident. Paul never left Tsu's side, but still she didn't wake up. Her Uncle Jimmy, Aunt Shirley and Lily were there and Tsu's mother, Mrs. Monroe, had just arrived. In one moment she had been reading a letter from her daughter stating how happy and in love she was, and that she was moving to Philadelphia. In the next, she was receiving a telegram stating that Tsu was in the hospital. When Mrs. Monroe came across Paul, he looked absolutely wrecked. His hair was disheveled, his clothes were dingy, his limbs and face were scraped up, and he looked like he hadn't slept in days. She went over and embraced him.

"You must be, Paul. I'm Tsu's mama, Anna," she told him. Paul threw his arms around the thin older woman's waist and cried into her bosom. Mrs. Monroe was very conservative looking. She was a nice looking woman, but she didn't do much of anything to enhance her natural look. "I want to thank you for sparking the first bit of life I've heard in her for a long while. I read it, in her words and I can see it in your face now how much you mean to one anotha."

"I'm sorry for all of this ma'am. It's all my fault. She's lying here because I didn't protect her like I was supposed to," Paul sobbed.

"Hush now. I haven't known her to be happier. This is just a spell, child. She's got something to pull through for. Besides, I'm a firm believer in improbable relationships and know that higher powers are always at work." The two of them were instantly drawn to one another because of the love and the grief they felt for Tsu. "So tell me now, what's her condition?" Anna asked. They all began speaking on top of one another, as Anna greeted the rest of her family in the hospital room. She knelt over her sleeping daughter and said a small prayer, before kissing Tsu's forehead.

Moments later, a sophisticated looking colored doctor came in to address the family and to update them on Tsu's condition. As a well-respected member of the community, Jimmy had requested that the doctor leave out any evidence of gunplay. The family needed the medical record to support that all of her injuries were sustained from the fall and the ledge.

"Well folks we've done just about everything we can do for her here. Her heart's fine, she's breathing on her own, but she's sustained some pretty nasty blows to the head." The doctor pointed out Tsu's visible injuries. "The bruising across her face and the wound on her head, are most likely the reasons why she is still in the coma. When or if she comes out of it….is really up to her at this point," the doctor informed them. "And don't worry. We've patched up her shoulder as well. It looks to me like she may have slammed it into the ledge and a piece of it pierced into her as well. There will be minimal scarring in time. It's all in the report." The doctor hesitated before continuing. "However, there is another matter I would like to discuss with the family though," he added.

"Paul! Need to have a word witcha," Sheriff Bingham approached the grief stricken group of visitors from behind. Rudely interrupted the colored doctor in mid-sentence. He smugly looked into the faces of the family members, and the staff in the hospital. "Was told I might fine ya here, son. It's urgent bizness," the sheriff enforced. He continued to look around the colored hospital in disgust.

"It's alright, Paul. You go with this nice man and I will tend to Tsu. You look like you could use a break." Anna remembered Bingham the moment she saw him from her younger years in Lexington. She recalled how much he loved to torment coloreds with that mean mutt of his, while she was growing up. She didn't want him anywhere around her daughter. She knew what kind of man he really was, and no justice for color folks was ever going to happen while he resided in office.

"Excuse me for a moment. I 'll be right back," he explained to Mrs. Monroe. Paul left Tsu's bedside and walked down the long corridor with the Sheriff, back towards the entrance. Paul was confident that the intrusion had nothing to do with Tsu's accident being investigated. So, he thought that it would be in their best interest if he cooperated with Sheriff Bingham.

"What can I do for you, Sheriff Bingham?" Paul asked. "Can't you see I'm a little busy at the moment?" he added. He also didn't want to raise any suspension by being *to* cooperative.

"Can ya tell me how ya got those scratches and bruises on yur face, neck and arms, son?" The sheriff pointed to several visible markings on Paul's body.

"It really is all a blur, sheriff, but I suppose they're from the ledge and carrying Tsu through the woods. I didn't have the use of my arms while I made my way through the woods to get her to the hospital. I haven't even paid much mind to the scratches." Paul hadn't given much thought to his own appearance. He had been to concern with concealing any evidence that could suggest that Tsu's accident was more than just that.

"Is dat so? Would dis accident have occurred out at Hawk's Ledge, son?" Sheriff Bingham proceeded as if he was trying to snare Paul in a trap.

"That would be correct, sir." Paul knew that the sheriff was intentionally dragging out his line of questioning. Perhaps hoping that Paul would break under the pressure, so Paul cut to the chase. "What is all this pertaining to, sir? I was right in the middle of something." The Sheriff looked pensively into Paul's smoky eyes, trying to measure his character. He placed a wade of chew into his mouth before speaking.

"It seems that Willy J. Baker went off missin' bout three days back. Lil' Johnny Sampson found his body early dis mornin' in da woods behind our baseball field." Paul interrupted.

"What do you mean his body? William's in Savannah." Paul acted confused. Sheriff Bingham took a long look at him, as he continued to chew his tobacco.

"He came back early fo' some reason. It appears, dat William might've gotten hisself drunk and stumbled into a wasp nest. His face and limbs were so swell up from all the bites, we hardly

184

recognized him. Not to mention the wildlife dat had been feastin' on his remains da past few days." Sheriff Bingham spat out some of his chew on the hospital floor, before closing in on Paul. "You have any idea why William mighta been out at those fields, son?" Paul steadied himself before he spoke. He needed to be convincing.

"Honestly Sheriff, I have no idea why Willy would've been at the fields. I didn't even know he was back from his honeymoon." Paul pushed his whirly hair back from off of his face. He appeared distressed by the news the sheriff had just given him. "He was my best friend. The only friend I had left in town," Paul expelled.

"I spoke to Abby dis mornin' and she said he left her in Savannah a few days back. Somethin' bout he had some bizness to atten' to. You know what he mighta been referrin' to?" Bingham questioned.

"Sheriff, I have no idea. I have nothing to do with Willy's business affairs." He looked even more distressed. "I haven't even talk to him since the wedding. I wonder what would've made him come back early and why the field." Tears welled up in his eyes. They were easy for him to produce because he was so concerned about Tsu's condition. Backing off a bit, the sheriff continued on with his interrogation.

"Now this lil' Niglet of yurs got into an accident the same night William went missin', if I'm not mistaken." Sheriff Bingham's eyes were pressing. Paul didn't like how the sheriff referred to Tsunami and his expression told the sheriff as much.

"Tsu," Paul emphasized," and I were swimming at the creek and she slipped off the cliff and hit her head and body against the ledge, Sheriff. I haven't seen Willy since his wedding day. I've kinda had my own shit to deal with over the past week now, haven't I, sir?" Paul protested. The Sheriff just gave him a side smile and spat another wade of chew on the shiny white floor.

"I myself have found that I've been caught under a nigger woman's spell before. Once ya get dat scent in ya, it's intoxicatin', isn't it?" Paul didn't respond, but he didn't like where the sheriff was going with the conversation. "Dat niglet of yurs is quite a piece, I'll give ya dat. I can see why ya all twitte-pated wit her. Maybe, just maybe, your pal Willy had a thing wit her as well and things got outta hand between you two. From what I understand, the darkies were always more his thang than yurs, if I'm not mistaken?" Bingham posed. Paul was furious, but he knew that the sheriff was trying to rile him up in order to get him to reveal any shred of evidence that William's and Tsu's accidents were connected.

"No, Sheriff. Tsu has been mine and mine alone. Last I knew, William was happily married and away. Whatever business he had to attend to at the field, I assure you had nothing to do with us," Paul countered. He wanted nothing more than to strike Bingham for implicating that Tsu was involved with William in any way. But he couldn't give him a reason to arrest or detain him. It was obvious that Bingham had suspicions. If he were put into custody, Paul might've found that he'd be the next one to have an accident, at the hands of the sheriff.

"Well, just wanted to make sure dat there was no foul play involved. I know how much it mighta upset ya knowin' that someone could be responsible for harmin' yur best friend and all. I do believe yur right, son. He mighta been the only frien' you had left in town, except for the coloreds dat is." Sheriff Bingham momentarily paused. "Oh, and it might be in yur best int'rest for ya to stay away from Hawk's Ledge from here on out. You are the unluckiest kinda bastard when it comes to that place, and niggers are the ones that keep seemin' to get hurt cause of it." Bingham poked him one last time, hoping to get a rise out of him. It took everything that Paul had not to hit the sheriff. Sheriff Bingham took one last look around the colored hospital's entry way and sighed. "It sure does stink in here," he remarked before exiting the hospital.

Paul kept his cool but he wasn't sure if he had been convincing enough for the sheriff. He was pretty sure that Willy wouldn't have confided in anyone about his grand plans for Tsu and him. William had done a great job at keeping that dark side of himself hidden from all of them. Paul only knew about his abusive sexual tendencies, on account that he spent more time in Green Hill and had seen Willy's handy-work first hand on the girls there.

~   ~   ~   ~   ~

Paul thought back on what the sheriff had said. Stumbled into a wasp nest. Paul envisioned the six angry colored men finding William in the woods. Each of them able to get a lick or two in for the

187

sake of their daughters, before hurling that angry wasp nest at Willy J. Asphyxiation must've been instantaneous from the multiple stings he sustained, seeing how just one sting was lethal enough to kill him. When Jimmy had gotten to the hospital that night, he didn't say a word to Paul about what had happened. He just gave him a nod, which Paul returned. It was understood that William had been taken can of, even without Paul knowing any of the details. He needed to look shocked when the news was told to him. He now hoped, that for their sakes, his plan had worked.

~   ~   ~   ~   ~

After impatiently pacing in circles, waiting for the sheriff to leave, Lily ran over to Paul. She tugged on his shirt and he bent down to her. She whispered into his ear and his face took on a new expression. He hurriedly walked back over to the colored doctor.

"Can she be moved?" he questioned the man responsible for his beloved Tsunami's care.

"I don't see why not. She's is stable and like I said earlier, we've done all we can do for her here," the doctor replied. "I think it's best if the family starts thinking about more permanent arrangements for her."

Chapter Fourteen

Philadelphia was a lovely place enriched with culture, opportunity and history. Paul had obtained a lovely four bedroom home on the outskirts of the city. He was doing extremely well with the professorship position he had procured back when he was in Lexington.

Sunlight poured into the bedroom windows as Paul was getting dress in his dungarees, to do his Saturday morning yard work. Tsu slowly began opening her heavy eyes. She observed a man, resembling Paul undressing by his dresser. His beard was fuller, and he looked slightly different, but she knew it was the man that she loved.

"Paul," she said, her voice soft from disuse. She, tried to push her weakened body into a more upright position on the bed.

Had he been dreaming? Was his mind beginning to play tricks on him? Paul turned his attentions to the bed where Tsu had been sleeping, and found her awakened and talking. He hastily approached the bed and fell to his knees grasping her hand. His eyes welled up with tears.

"Tsu, you've come back to me." He kissed her hand several times in disbelief. Tsu wasn't really sure what Paul was talking about, so she simply smiled and asked him.

"What on earf ya talkin' bout Paul? Where I been?" she playfully asked. She immediately became confused why she had spoken such bad English. The pronunciation and sentence structure did not come out quite right. Pushing up on his elbows, Paul drew in closer to Tsu's face.

"Tsu, you've been in a coma for eight years. It's 1969.

Tsu was taken aback by what he had told her and she began to cry with Paul. She was confused and didn't quite understand what was happening.

"Eight year? I los' eight year life?" Tsu was horrified that another man had stolen another chunk of her life away. The last thing she could actually recall, was running away from William at the cabin and getting shot. Tsu continued to cry while Paul begin filling her in with all of the events that had occurred after she fell over the cliff that night. He told her about William and his death. He also explained to her that there could be some delay in her brain activity due to her being in a coma for so long. This was the reason why her speech and phrases were not forming quite as correctly as she was accustomed to. Once Tsu had calmed down a little more and was somewhat able to comprehend all that Paul had told her, he rose to his feet in haste.

"Wait here a minute. I almost forgot," Paul insisted, as if she could go anyway. The muscles in her legs had atrophied, due to the fact that she had not used them in so many years. Paul jetted out of the bedroom and down the hall, yelling "Momma!" Who was he talking too? Tsu remembered that he had told her that his parents had died when he was ten. Who was he referring too now? Her mind felt jumbled, trying to understand things. Running back up the hall and through the doorway, Tsu heard and then saw her mother walking through the bedroom door.

"I don't believe it. My baby's finally awake. It's a miracle!" Anna Monroe cried out, overjoyed and ecstatic, from seeing her long lost child awoken from her slumber. "Praise the lord!" More tears streamed down her face at the sight of her mother. She looked much older than the last time Tsu had seen her. It was indeed true. She had been asleep for about a decade by the look of her mother. And if Tsu wasn't overwhelmed enough, Paul interrupted them presenting a little girl in front of her.

"And this little miracle, is our daughter." Tsu was distraught and even more confused. It had just been August in 1961 and now it was 1969, and somehow she was a mother. She wondered how all this was possible. The small seven year old child ran up to the bed throwing her lanky arms around her mother.

"I've missed you, Momma," the girl remarked, her eyes bursting with tears. Tsu looked into her face and it had resembled her own in some ways, except for that magnificent curly hair. It was definitely influenced by her father. Tsu thought, how can this be? Asleep for eight years and now I'm a mother! Paul could see how perplexed she was.

"You were a couple weeks pregnant when William attacked us. The fact that our baby survived that attack, the fall and the coma, makes her, and you, pretty remarkable, I'd say."

"Miracles," Mrs. Monroe interjected.

Examining the girl's face with her fingers, she asked, "Wats yur name?" Talking was frustrating to her. She knew what and how she wanted to sound but her mouth or her brain would not cooperate.

"My name's Tempest, Momma," she answered.

Tsu immediately looked to Paul, overwrought with her emotions from the news of the day. 'The Tempest' was a storm and the title of a Shakespearian play.

"Paul! How could ya name her anotha natural saster?" she inquired with frustration. Not only by the name he'd given their child, but with also her speech. Paul stood in the doorway and only laughed.

"We have a lifetime to debate over that my beautiful, Tsunami." Paul joined the others around the bed in celebration, for Tsu had returned to them.

~   ~   ~   ~   ~

The next several weeks were spent on Tsu's therapy and catching her up on all that happened while she slept. Tsu became reacquainted with Lily, who was now twenty-two and a school teacher in the city of Philadelphia. She came to visit every chance she got. She had grown up so lovely. She was sophisticated, slender and beautiful. Far from that sassy child Tsu had just known. On her left ring finger, Lily still wore the diamond and gold ring Paul had given her all those years ago.

"Are ya marry now, Lily?" Tsu wondered seeing how she had missed out on so much.

"Not yet. I've got a career to worry about first. There was a fella in my life but..." Lily hesitated. "You and Paul have ruined me. How could I ever be in love with anyone other than you two? Could I ever know anything even remotely close to what you guys have?"

"Lily, it also cos' us a lot. Eight years is a long time to lose. I'm so angry and bitta, and I feel so out of place here. Almos' like I don't belong here. And my words, Lily. You know my words defined me and I barely get 'em right." Tsu paused out of irritation. "I 'magine that it must've been much worse for all of ya to go through day after day and year after year. Everythin' for me was just yestaday, but things so vastly diff'rent. Our lives have completely change because we fell in love."

"You don't have to feel out of place, by any means. You are exactly where you are supposed to be and with the people you are supposed to be with. It's going to take some time, but you keep practicing every day and you will get better and better. Remember that lesson? Just yesterday you told me that." Lily looked adoringly at Tsu and she understood what Lily was doing. She also understood that what she had found with Paul, was a once in a lifetime kind of love, only very few people got to experience. Lily was just so happy that she got to be a part of such a beautiful thing.

"Lily, you can find what we had too. Just gotta get yur nose out of the books, like I did, and look round once in a while," Tsu teased.

"You mean to say what you two have," Lily insisted. But Tsu meant to say had. She didn't really feel as connected to Paul as she once did. She felt more as an embarrassing obligation, or a burden to her family. Not wanting to raise any other additional concerns from Lily, Tsu changed the subject.

"I think ya mighta jinxed me, Lily," Tsu snickered. She wanted to lighten the mood.

"How do you mean?" Lily inquired.

"I faintly member ya saying' somethin' like I was so much high on love, the only way down, was to get shot out of the sky. That's 'xactly what happened," Tsu laughed.

"Tsu! That's not funny." Lily tried to hold back her laughter, but could not contain it. The two of them laughed and enjoyed each other's company as they had done in the past. They were sisters again.

~   ~   ~   ~   ~

As Lily was getting ready to pull out, Paul and Mrs. Monroe pulled into the driveway.

"Hey Lily, how'd it go today?" Paul inquired.

"Afternoon, Paul." She kissed him and then Mrs. Monroe on the cheek. "It went well. She is resting now, but she seems stronger and her speech improves every time I see her."

"That's good news." He hesitated. "How is she with you? She's kinda distant with me and even Tempest is starting to notice it.

194

It's difficult for a little girl to understand why her mother isn't...well maternal towards her."

"This is all still very new to her. I wouldn't worry about it, her motherly instincts are bound to kick in," Lily explained. "We've all got to be patient and understanding. Tsu's not only has to relearn how to walk and talk. She is also struggling with losing so many years of her life, where so much has changed." Paul and Mrs. Monroe listened eagerly. "However, she did mention something about feeling out of place and being bitter and angry about what happened. If anything, you might wanna start there," she concluded.

"Don't you two pay no mind to it. That's my child in there and I shoulda done somethin' bout her self-esteem long ago. Ima give her a lil' bit longer and Ima talk to her and fix all this self-pity nonsense. Didn't wait all these years for her to wake up, just to watch her destroy herself. You'll see. Mama will fix it."

"Yes, ma'am!" This was Paul's only response. He was smart enough by now to know when to get on board with Mrs. Monroe.

"Well, it sounds like everything will be just fine here." Lily smiled at Paul. "I'll be back next weekend." She kissed the both of them once again, but this time, goodbye.

~   ~   ~   ~   ~

Mrs. Monroe spent hours every day assisting Tsu with her physical therapy and helping her regain her ability to walk. After several months of therapy, Tsu was managing quite well. After the

195

accident, Paul had asked Mrs. Monroe to move to Philadelphia with them to help him take care of Tsu. After all she was a nurse, but as her mother she could do nothing less for her child.

Mrs. Monroe could sense Tsu's apprehension with her place with Paul and Tempest, and all that had occurred in Lexington that summer. She couldn't help her own strong maternal desire to console her child. She wanted to make her feel better about herself and to accept another truth. A truth beside the one that she so heavily clung too. She had to show Tsu a different viewpoint, if the family was going to make it.

"Baby, the time has come for me to be movin' on. I'll be leaving tomorrow in the morning," Mrs. Monroe stated.

"What do you mean, Momma?" Tsu's face tensed with fear. The thought of being alone in that house with Paul and Tempest, frightened her.

"Momma's much older now baby, and it's time for me to retire. Mrs. Ellington resides in her townhouse in New York now. I am going to move in with her and live out the rest of my days with my best friend, and in style. Besides you can't have two useless cooks in one household tryin' to manage a kitchen," Mrs. Monroe joked.

"Momma...I'm really not ready. What if I can't make this work? What if Tempest resents me cause I not what she's been told I am? I'm so much less now." Tears streamed down Tsu's face, but Mrs. Monroe was ready to combat them.

"Lily told me a while back, that you've been doubting yurself and yur place within this family," Anna stated.

"Momma. I love him and you. All that you've done and Tempest is 'mazing, but somehow...I don't feel like I deserve any of it. Any of you guys."

"Ya haven't felt worthy of anythang good most of yur life, child." Mrs. Monroe took a deep breath in. "You know, Tsu, your father was the best man I knew, but you somehow managed to find yourself a better one. And he can cook," she added. "Paul loves you like nothing I've ever seen, child," she told Tsu while helping her walk across the room. "He made a place for the four of us, sheltered and protected you, even exercised your legs almost every single morning while you were in that coma. He never lost hope that you would find your way back to us, and ya did." Tsu listened carefully to her mother's words. "I know you think that your name was some kind of curse. Your father, God rest his soul, chose that name because of its strength, not its devastation. He wanted you to feel and to be powerful, like you truly are."

"Momma, look at all the trouble I caused, in Lexington and in Paul's life. I have been by the very definition, devastating to them as well as myself," Tsu assured her.

"Oh, pish posh, Tsu. You ain't destroyed nothin' that wasn't broke in the first place. You were a part of change, Tsu, for the better," Mrs. Monroe confessed. "You and Paul fell in love right smack in the middle of one of this nation's biggest social movements of our times. And against all odds...you won. That boy who tried to kill the two of you was the devastation. And Lexington hasn't been the same since. That's a good thing. Segregation barriers began to break down even more. Color folks began starting up more and more businesses. And the children, Tsu. The colored children began pursuing their education, baby. Your story became a legend simply because of the extraordinary woman you are, and by not accepting your place. Everyone knows it, Tsu. Especially Paul. From the very moment he met you in the street that day, he could tell how special you were." Tsu's eyes were full as her mother bombarded Tsu with her words.

"Why do I attract so much bad then, Momma?" She wrapped her arms around her mother's small back and tears streamed down her face.

"Everyone just always wanted to be around you, child. Both the good and the bad. Which can be difficult to figure out which is which and who is what, but you draw people to you. You're like a warm, radiant, light in the darkness. Some seek out the light to be a part of it. Others seek it out to blot out its existence. Even still, evil in its purest forms has tried hard to put you out, and yet you still manage to rise and let your light shine. Whew, if that ain't some kinda power girl, I don't know what is." Tsu listened intently to her mother as they continued their laps across the living room floor. "Lily told me that you referred to yourself as a shell of a person after that man raped you all those years ago. But, hear me now and hear me good. That's nothin' but a lie. If anythang you let yourself become a dim lit ember, but once tended to, you returned to flame. Own who you are baby, give it to the world and for heaven's sake, build on it with that man and your daughter who love you so very much."

~ ~ ~ ~ ~

It's amazing how restorative a mother's words can be to their children, even as an adult. Mother's words can rebuild our very spirits just as easily as they can tear them apart. Tsu made a conscious decision that day, not to think of herself or Tempest as disasters, or feel like she was a burden to Paul. It would be a difficult transition for her, but she was willing to put in the effort. Paul had the courage to love her, risking and forfeiting his entire way of life. Since she loved him back, he created this new life for their family.

~ ~ ~ ~ ~

A few nights later, Paul and Tsu decided to take a walk after dinner. They brought along Tempest and their dog Macbeth, a husky St. Bernard. Mrs. Monroe had been gone a few days and Tsu had found that the adjustment wasn't as difficult as she had thought it would be. She just needed to open herself up to them.

"I'm sorry I've been so distant. I really am workin' on comin' to terms that I am worthy of all of this and you guys," she explained.

"I know you are. I wish you could see yourself through our eyes. You're so much more than I could've hope for. I'm here for you and I will do whatever it takes for you to understand what you mean to us."

"I believe you will, Paul. Not much seems to deter you from your objectives," she laughed.

"Nope! Not even your pigheadedness." He flashed her a smile.

"Me? Pigheaded? How dare you infer such a thing?" She pulled in closer to his arm, momentarily resting her head against him. Holding hands staring into the night sky Paul turned to Tsu.

"I have another surprise for you, Tsu," Paul explained.

"Another surprise! My birthday wish already came true."

"What birthday wish?" Paul was confused.

"The wish I made at your house, when you made me that yummy cake."

"Is that so? What did you wish for?"

"Can't tell ya," she teased.

"If it came true you can, Tsu" She toyed with the idea of keeping it to herself, but couldn't resist his inquisitive face.

"I wished for a life….with you." She blushed. "And after a lil' nap, I woke up, got a good scoldin' from my mother and found that I had one."

"A looooooong nap, Tsu. I'll have to remember to enlist your mother in the future, when you need some sense talked into you." He laughed. "Too bad you wasted your wish though. We already had a life together."

"I didn't know that at the time," she admonished. "So what other surprise could there possibly be," she questioned.

"Well, since you already got what you wanted....maybe I won't tell you," he teased.

"Come on, Paul? How can you deny me?" She pouted her lips and batted her eyes.

"Not fair. You and Tempest with that look. You two know that's my weakness," he admitted. "After the move, I found your journal, telling our story. I sent it off and got it published for you."

"Paul, you didn't." Tsu was mortified.

"I did, and it did pretty well for a short story. It being so scandalous for the times and all. Don't worry, I didn't add anything in the end about William. It's just our story. Just the way you left it. Except we lived happily ever after. I added that at the end." Tsu's face change at the mention of William's name and Paul noticed. "I'm sorry about William, Tsu, and that I didn't stop him or get to you earlier." Paul was still accepting the blame for his friend's actions. "I should've known that he was up to something. I just hoped that if I kept talking to William about love, forgiveness, God...he would've changed how he was. I loved him and I wanted to help him be a better man."

"Shhhhhhh. You were there when it counted. And none of us could've known what he was plannin'. You thought you were friends. What I can't figure out is the note that you received," Tsu pondered

"What do you mean?"

"Lily said that you said, it wasn't in William's handwritin'. Was he skilled enough to fake a completely different hand?" Tsu asked.

"Maybe. I wouldn't underestimate William or what he was capable of ever again. He was pretty clear that he was going to go after you. He said so the first time we saw you and once again during the July picnic. I just didn't know how far he was willing to go." Paul paused. "But enough about William." Paul had become distracted with thoughts of the Fourth of July picnic. "Do you remember the fireworks?" Embarrassed, she blushed at the thought. Of course she remembered it. It was only months ago to her.

"I do. You were quite the gentleman that night, if I recall correctly," she sarcastically replied. Paul laughed remembering how impetuous he had been.

"I thought I'd never seen anything so beautiful in all my life, as you in that dress. Of course I was wrong," he teased.

"Paul!" Tsu pushed him and he smiled.

"I'm sorry, but then Tempest was born and she stole that title away from you." They both looked to the happy little girl, dancing alongside them down the street. "Don't worry, you kinda got it back," he informed her.

"Really?" Tsu questioned. "And how did I do that?"

"Simple. You woke up. My three favorite girls crying and holding each other in our bedroom, is definitely the most beautiful thing I've ever seen," Paul confessed.

"Always so charmin', Mr. Morrison. One could think that you were out to take advantage of me in my vulnerable and weakened condition," Tsu posed. Paul raised his brow and bit on his lip.

"Maybe that has been my intention all along, Mrs. Morrison." Tsu raised her own brow.

"Are we married, Mr. Morrison? Unless priest are now willin' to marry comatose victims, I do not recall saying I do." Tsu provoked him.

"Technically, not yet. But we can rectify that little matter this weekend. Unless you want to keep living in sin, that is?" Paul teased.

"I'm not sure if I'm ready for marriage. After all, we've only just met," Tsu replied, batting her eyelashes at him.

"Tsu....we have a seven year old daughter. I think we're overdue," Paul's response was more serious this time.

"That we do," she sounded, looking into Tempest's joyful face. "Next weekend would be mighty fine. Now take me home, slave. I've grown weary on our walk." Paul laughed at Tsu. Scooping her up, he carried her back to their home. This was the playful Tsunami he had remembered.

~   ~   ~   ~   ~

They returned home and Paul tucked Tempest into bed after reading her, her favorite bedtime story, Cinderella. When he returned back to his and Tsu's bedroom, Tsu was wearing one of his white T-shirts with the collar cut off.

"I also member this," Tsu taunted him.

"As do I," Paul added, closing the door behind him. He hadn't seen his Tsunami like this for such a long time. Heat built up in his body as it had done so many times before for her. Stripping his clothes to the floor, he walked over to the bed scooping Tsu up in his arms. Kissing across her collarbone he whispered. "May I have you?"

Tsu smiled. Some men do ask, she thought.

"You already have me." She pulled Paul down atop of her on the bed and his hands began reacquainting themselves with her flesh.

"Remember, Tsu? Nice and slow at first. I don't want to hurt you," he stated through labored breathing.

"I remember," she replied in the same labored state. "Thank you for loving me, so much, Paul," she expressed with sincerity. Paul hesitated in his advancement then kissed her passionately on the mouth. Looking lovingly into her face he replied.

"Thank you for giving me everything I've wanted in life. You are my home." Overcome with both love and lust, the two of them submerged once again into the ecstasy they had once known.

The End.

44191461R00115